AS TIME GOES BY

When Lally caretakes her grand-mother's croft in the wildest part of Scotland, she fully expects that she'll return soon, to a high-powered job in Edinburgh. Her scatterbrained sister Bel has other plans though, and Lally quickly finds the people and the place seeping into her soul. Or is it just one person, in the shape of new neighbour Iain? Torn between two worlds, Lally's decision will not only impact on herself, but also on everyone else around her.

GILLIAN VILLIERS

AS TIME GOES BY

Complete and Unabridged

LINFORD
Leicester

First published in Great Britain in 2011

First Linford Edition
published 2012

British Library CIP Data

Villiers, Gillian.
    As time goes by. - -
    (Linford romance library)
    1. Love stories.
    2. Large type books.
    I. Title II. Series
    823.9'2–dc23

    ISBN 978–1–4448–1291–6

Published by
F. A. Thorpe (Publishing)
Anstey, Leicestershire

Set by Words & Graphics Ltd.
Anstey, Leicestershire
Printed and bound in Great Britain by
T. J. International Ltd., Padstow, Cornwall

This book is printed on acid-free paper

A Stranger Arrives

'Lal, I think someone's coming to Harbour House. I think it must be Sandy's nephew at last! And isn't it great he's seeing it on a good day?'

Lal adjusted the lamb she was holding between her knees and inserted the feeding bottle into its mouth. 'Are you sure it isn't just another day tripper having a mooch around?' In the summer months the sisters were all too familiar with the friendly, but sometimes intrusive curiosity of those who visited this remote northern corner of Scotland.

'It's not,' said Bel triumphantly. 'He's got a key to the gate!'

'Ah,' said Lal. They had waited a long time for this mysterious nephew of Sandy's to put in an appearance. He hadn't seemed in any hurry to get here.

Lal let the lamb finish the last of the milk and then went over to stand beside

1

her sister at the drystone wall. From here they had a good view down to the wide bay below.

There was a very smart four-by-four parked at the gate to Harbour House, and sure enough the man beside it had a key to the padlock. By now he had driven the car through the gate and was locking it behind him. Goodness, did he really think he needed to do that? If Gran had had her way the whole place would have been left open. No-one usually locked things around here, but the solicitor had insisted.

Lally smiled to herself as she thought of what this smart stranger would make of Harbour House. House was actually a bit of a grand title. The original place might once have been the biggest building in the hamlet, but it hadn't really been more than a three-bedroomed cottage with a few outbuildings. Now, apart from the Bothy, the whole place was derelict.

'He'll probably take one look and run a mile,' she said hopefully. She had already taken a dislike to the nephew. He had never shown any interest in Sandy, and then he had left it so long to come and view his inheritance. She was sure he wasn't her kind of person.

'Huh,' replied Bel, hopping from one skinny leg to the other in her excitement. 'Think of the hundreds of visitors who've been to our door to ask if the place is for sale. Everybody who sees it loves it. He'll be no different.'

'I'm not sure it's your average city-dweller's idea of a dream home.' Lally didn't know much about Sandy's great-nephew, except that he lived in London. And even from this distance, his clothes, like his car, looked shiny and out of place.

'I think I'll go down and say hello,' said Bel, already turning to leave. With Bel, to think was to act.

'Maybe he won't want . . . '

'He'll have loads of questions. Of course he'll want someone to answer them.'

Lally watched her sister skipping

across the field. It was good to see her with some energy again, although Lal wasn't sure their new neighbour would be too impressed with his visitor. In her ancient shorts and baggy T shirt, with a scarf tied over her bushy hair, she looked much younger than fourteen. He would think he was being visited by a minute village tramp. Lal smiled again. Too bad. He might as well get to know Bel now as later, she certainly wasn't going to leave him in peace.

She turned back to see how many lambs still needed to be fed. It looked like she would be finishing the job on her own.

★ ★ ★

Iain couldn't believe he'd wasted a week's precious holiday to come here. He'd known the place was a dump, but the solicitor had spoken of 'potential'. He should have guessed, when the old fusspot had been unable, or unwilling, to send some photographs, that the visit to Harbour House was going to be a disaster.

He parked the hired vehicle before a rickety gate. Thank goodness he'd opted for a four-wheel-drive with a track like this! The only new thing in sight was the padlock, which fortunately opened the minute he inserted the similarly shiny key. Not that he was in any great hurry to get through the gate and look around. The place was just a total mess.

Even from here he could see the house was uninhabitable. It didn't seem to have a roof. How on earth had Great-uncle Alexander lived here for so many years? He hadn't really been in touch with the rest of the family for decades, so Iain didn't know the answer to that question.

Closing the gate carefully behind him, he followed the track to the left and up the slight rise away from the coast. Now he could see the house at close quarters and it definitely had no roof. It wasn't just that the slates were missing, there weren't even any rafters! The place was a total disaster. After wandering around for a moment or two, he realised there were all manner of buildings here scattered about in no particular order. And some of these looked in better shape than the house. Actually, there was one that looked almost promising.

This was a stone building standing at right angles to the ruined house. It had a roof that looked fairly new. And windows with glass in them. Now, this was a bit better.

He was peering through one of these glazed windows when he heard footsteps behind him. He jerked upright and looked around. You didn't expect trouble in the back of beyond, but you couldn't be too careful.

'I see you've arrived,' said a diminutive figure dressed in what Iain first thought were rags. Then he realised they were a crumpled T shirt and rather dirty shorts. He thought the figure was a girl, although he couldn't be quite sure, the hair being covered by a kind of gypsy scarf.

'Er, hello,' he said.

'And hello to you too. I presume you're Sandy's great-nephew, the one he left his house to?'

The girl, for it was definitely a girl, stood before him with her hands on slim hips, her freckled face beaming at him expectantly. He didn't reply immediately. He wasn't used to being accosted by youngsters of this age, and certainly not with friendly intent.

She obviously thought he needed a little prompting and thrust out a small, freckled hand. 'I'm Bel Dunmore. We're your nearest neighbours, Tigh na Mara, the croft over there. How do you do?'

At that Iain had to smile, despite himself. He didn't like people who were too forward, but the child was doing her best to make him welcome.

He bent to shake her hand gravely and said, 'Iain Cunningham, pleased to meet you.'

The girl retrieved her hand and put it

back on her hip, surveying him with the keen interest of someone much older. 'And you are Sandy's great-nephew, yes? We've been waiting ages for you to appear. Gran said we should give you time and Lally said you probably weren't interested and were going to sell the place. Is she right?'

Iain reverted to his first opinion. This child was far too inquisitive.

'I've been busy,' he said repressively. 'And now, if you don't mind, I'm going to have a look around.'

He took the keys from his pocket, meaning this as a sign of dismissal, but the waif couldn't take a hint.

She leaned forward to examine the collection of keys in his hand. 'Do you want me to help you? I'll be able to recognise the key for the Bothy if you let me look properly, and then you probably shouldn't go into the hay barn on your own, Billy and his men always meant well but they never got round to finishing the upper level and . . . '

Iain jangled the keys quickly when

she paused for breath. At least if she could identify the one for this little place, it would be a start.

'This is the Bothy, is it?'

'That's right. See, this big brass key is for the door here. The name was Sandy's joke. I mean, this was the bothy, you know, for the itinerant workers in the summer, but he could have called it anything, it being so smart once he'd done it up, but he said once a bothy always a bothy and . . . '

Iain turned the key in the lock and reached over the girl's head to push the door open. It swung heavy but true on its hinges and for the first time he felt a stirring of interest. He didn't believe a place like this could be smart, but it smelled dry and clean and as the door swung wider he saw how the light flooded in.

The girl's expression was rapt as she looked at him, then inside, then at him again.

'It's so cool, isn't it?' she said, sounding for the first time like the teenager she presumably was. 'Come and have a look.'

He should have been irritated, this was his property, not hers, but he found himself carried along by her enthusiasm.

They entered the long room and he looked about. When he'd peered in through the window all he had been able to make out was a settee and a wood-burning stove. Now he saw that the downstairs was basically one large room, with a kitchen at one end and the living area at the other. The floor was a pale wood and in the gable facing the sea was a massive window that gave the most amazing view over the rocks and water to the mountains beyond.

'Sandy lived in a caravan for years whilst he did this up. Said he knew how he wanted it and it was going to be just right. There's a small bathroom at the back here, see, and then the bedroom is on the platform up there. The stairs look steep but they designed so they're really easy to get up and down, I'll show you.'

True to her word the child ran up what looked like a broad wooden ladder with a rail on one side.

'Come and have a look.'

Iain shrugged and obeyed. He thought there wouldn't be much space up here but the roof must be higher than he realised. He could stand up easily. From the two sky lights, one facing each way, he had views of the road down which he had come and of the cliffs to the west. Stunning.

'It's a shame you didn't tell us you were coming, we could have aired the place and had the bed made up for you,' continued his guide. 'Didn't the solicitor give you our number? I'm sure Gran asked him to.'

'He may have done . . . ' Iain hadn't for a moment considered phoning strangers and telling them of his plans. What was it to them? He hadn't even told his London neighbours he was moving to Edinburgh and he had no intention of introducing himself to his Edinburgh neighbours when he moved in. That's what he liked about cities, you could keep yourself to yourself. Whereas here . . .

'Never mind. I'll show you where the bedding is and I can help you do it now if you want? Good job the weather's so nice, it shouldn't be damp. Actually, Sandy had this place so well insulated it hardly does get damp, not like Gran's place. Lally says she needs to do something about the heating there, but Gran says people have lived with nothing but peat fires for centuries and she's lucky to have the odd storage heater. Old people can be so awkward, can't they?'

'Ah . . . ' Iain didn't think he actually knew any old people. None of his grandparents were still alive and the Information Technology industry where he worked was a very young profession.

'Won't someone be wondering where you are?' he said, trying to be repressive. The child was already opening a wide cupboard and sorting out sheets. Really, it was a bit intrusive.

'No, Lally knows I'm here. We saw your car arrive. She would probably have come down too, but she had the lambs to feed.'

'And Lally is?'

'My sister. She's really Alicia, but everyone calls her Lally. Mum says it's a shame, with the lovely names she gave her children, that we insist on abbreviations. Lally, Ant and Bel which actually I think are much nicer than Alicia, Anthony and Annabel, don't you?'

Iain shrugged. He found himself on one side of the bed, catching the sheet as she shook it out towards him. If she insisted on helping he supposed he might as well make use of her. He might glean some local information from her, too.

'And all of you live here, in the, er, croft, do you?'

'No. I wish. The croft is Gran's, she's been running it on her own since Grampie died five years ago. I usually live in Glasgow, but Gran's sister had an operation last month and Gran's gone to look after her and Lal and I have come to croft-sit. Actually, I've been here a while, I had glandular fever and they said I needed to recuperate. It's been brilliant, I love it here!'

The child seemed to be irredeemably positive. Iain thought he'd heard glandular fever wasn't at all pleasant, but the girl, Bel, just beamed at the thought of the extra holiday it had gained for her.

'So that's why you're not at school?'

'Well, I wouldn't be today, would I, it being Saturday? But you're right, on week days I should be. I'm pretty much better now, but they'd said ages ago I should stay off until the end of the summer term which is brilliant. Right, that's the bed done. Do you want to come up and see Lally now? I'm sure she'd like to meet you.'

'Actually, I was hoping to have a look around here,' said Iain.

'Of course. Do you want me to show you?'

'On my own.' Iain decided if he didn't assert himself now he'd never get rid of the child. 'Off you go. You know, you're far too friendly, you shouldn't just talk to strangers like this.'

'But you're not a stranger, you're Sandy's great-nephew.' The girl looked at him as if he was stupid. 'I've had an idea. Why don't you come and eat with us later on? You won't want to cook the first night, even if you have brought food, and Lal always makes enough for ten. She won't mind.'

Eventually, just to get rid of the child, Iain found himself agreeing.

The Inheritance

'So?' said Lal when Bel reappeared. She was washing all the paraphernalia used in feeding the lambs. You didn't need to sterilise these things as you did for human babies, but it still took forever. She wished Gran wasn't so keen to take in the motherless lambs the other crofters couldn't be bothered with. 'I presume you got talking to him since you've been away so long. What's he like?'

'Tall, dark hair, southern English accent, lovely eyes. Didn't seem to like the other buildings much but he was impressed by the Bothy.'

'Of course,' said Lally. 'Who wouldn't be?' Sandy had done a marvellous job there, anyone would see that. 'So is he staying long?'

'I didn't get the chance to ask him, but you can do that this evening. I invited him to eat with us.'

Bel grinned, giving her sister the benefit of the full mouth of metal braces,
and disappeared before Lal could object
to the invitation. Actually, Lal had been
meaning to go down later on herself to
welcome the new neighbour. She would
no doubt have invited him for a meal.
That was what Gran would expect, would
have done if she was home. Still, it was
rather annoying having Bel impose it on
her like that.

She wondered what the man had
made of Bel. She was a little — unusual.
Lal loved her sister to bits but even she
could see that being so chatty and organising and curious about the world wasn't
normal teenager behaviour. Lal had certainly never been like that, and Ant, the
brother who came between them, cared
about nothing but his music, sailing,
and how best to keep himself enter-
tained. Which was why he had departed
on a month-long trip with the Sea Cadets
as soon as he'd finished his exams, therefore being totally unavailable to help on
the croft.

Lal sighed. Not that he would have been much help. He didn't like animals, and although he was perfectly happy to exercise himself to exhaustion doing press ups and forced marches or whatever they did in Cadets, somehow doing household chores always seemed to be too much hard work.

Fortunately Bel wasn't at all like that. Although she had missed lamb-feeding because she was so desperate to meet the new neighbour, you could never accuse her of being lazy. Looking out of the window, Lal could see her sister now hanging out the washing. She hurried out to help her. Bel was still convalescing and it was important she didn't do too much.

* * *

'I hope he's not vegetarian,' observed Bel as she watched her sister put the lamb casserole back in the oven.

'So do I,' said Lal. She hadn't even thought of that. No-one around here was vegetarian, in fact, the menfolk would probably rather die than consider it, but maybe Londoners were different? 'And what time are we expecting him? Did you say a time?'

'Not at first. I didn't think about it. But I popped back down when you were having a shower and suggested about seven.' Bel nodded. 'I didn't want him to worry about when to appear.'

'Thoughtful of you. Pity you didn't ask about his meat-eating tendencies.'

'I'll do him egg on toast if he refuses the casserole. Although I can't imagine he will. Everyone loves it.'

Lal wasn't sure everyone loved it, but she knew Bel did, which was one reason she had made it. It was so good to see the youngster eating properly again. She still looked like a skinny scarecrow, but at least her colour was coming back.

Lal went to try and tidy herself before the visitor arrived. She wasn't as thin as her sister, but they shared the same thick sandy hair which was so difficult to tame. Bel's favoured option of the moment was to cover hers in a gypsy scarf. Lal almost wished she could do the same, but instead scooped it back into a pony tail and put on a touch of make up. Gran always said if you made an effort you felt better yourself, and that was important. Not that Lal was nervous of this man or anything, but there was no harm in bolstering her spirits.

At precisely seven o'clock they saw him striding along the narrow road that skirted the bay.

'Punctual. That's good,' said Bel.

'He's very smartly dressed,' said Lal.

The visitor was a tall man with short dark hair, wearing dark trousers and what looked like a brand new shirt and jersey. Lal sighed as she glanced down at her own ancient jeans and hand-knitted multi-coloured cardigan. She could see they really weren't going to hit it off. She pulled open the little-used front door and smiled brightly.

'Iain Cunningham? Welcome to Strathan. I'm Lally.'

They shook hands and she ushered him into the conservatory, her gran's pride and joy. The views from here were magnificent, especially tonight with the late May sunshine catching the waves and turning them to silver.

The man commented politely on the scenery and said how kind it was of them to invite him over. Lal answered in a similar vein.

After ten minutes Bel had had enough of this. 'So,' she said brightly, showing all the metal on her teeth. 'Why did it take you so long to come and see Harbour House? It's nearly six months since Sandy died.'

Lal glared at her, more in hope than the expectation of having any effect.

'Er,' said the man, thrown by this direct approach.

'I'm sure you've been busy, down in London,' suggested Lal.

'Yes, I have.'

'You didn't even come to the funeral,' said Bel, her smile fading.

The man frowned. Lal wasn't surprised

he was put out. Bel really shouldn't show her disapproval, even if the locals had commented vocally on his absence.

'No,' said Iain. 'Actually, the funeral had already happened before I heard my uncle had died. You probably realise we weren't very close.'

'Yes, of course,' said Lally.

'Why weren't you close?' said Bel, spotting her opportunity. 'Sandy was lovely. He had masses of friends. We always wondered about his family.'

'Bel . . . ' said Lally, warningly.

To her surprise, after his initial shock, the man seemed to decide to take Bel at face value. Her curiosity was just that — an honest interest in the facts — and perhaps he sensed this. He said, 'To tell you the truth, I don't really know why we lost touch. Uncle Alexander — Sandy — was my grandfather's brother and it seemed they didn't get on. But I don't know the reasons why.'

'Didn't you ever ask?' said Bel, leaning forward, fascinated. She, of course, would have asked!

'It never really occurred to me. We lived down south, he moved up here after he left the Navy. Not all families stay in touch, you know.'

Bel shook her head disapprovingly. She had very strong feelings about family. In fact, about everything. Lal said quickly, 'I'll just check on the food. We'll eat in the kitchen, if that's all right?'

As she departed she heard Bel say, 'I hope you're not vegetarian, are you? Lal has made the most amazing lamb and barley casserole specially for you, but if you are I'm sure we can find something else.'

'No, I'm not vegetarian,' cut in Iain.

Lal grinned, pleased that he was going to eat what she had prepared, and that he had already realised the only way to get a word in when Bel was in full flow was to cut directly across her.

★　★　★

Iain hadn't expected to enjoy the evening. He wasn't a particularly sociable person

23

and when he did mix with others he preferred it to be people he knew well and was sure he liked. He would never have spent time with these two garishly dressed, sandy-haired sisters in his day-to-day life. And yet here, in the funny little kitchen with a young dog sleeping by the Rayburn, he listened to the way they teased and interrupted each other, and found himself intrigued.

'The food was delicious,' he said, as he finished a second plateful. 'No, no more, honestly.'

'I'm glad you appreciate Lal's food. She's a good cook,' said the youngster, willing as ever to give her opinion. 'Actually, she's good at everything she does.'

'No, I'm not,' said the older girl, looking embarrassed. Iain hadn't yet worked out how old she was, early twenties perhaps, but she had a composed and capable manner about her that supported her sister's assertion.

'Yes, you are. Good cook, superb

gardener, good with animals. And you got a two-one in your degree, so you're clever, too.' The child turned to give Iain the benefit of her broad smile. 'And she got a post with the National Museums of Scotland, straight out of uni, not many people can do that.'

'You work in a museum?' said Iain, confused. He was under the impression the sisters were living out here, at least for the summer.

'I had a one year placement, that's all. It was fun, very interesting, but it was due to end this month so when Gran needed to get away it suited me fine.'

'I was here already, as I said,' continued Bel. 'I really didn't want to go back to Glasgow and someone needed to look after the croft so it worked out perfectly.'

Lally nodded. 'Yes, it did. I suppose you could say I'm unemployed at the moment, but it's wonderful to be here in the summer, and I'm sure something will turn up.'

'It's, er, very lovely here,' said Iain, amazed at people who could be so laid back about their plans for life.

'Isn't it? So, we were wondering, are you planning to stay?' said Bel. She ignored the rather obvious kick her sister aimed at her. 'Or are you going to sell the Harbour House? I think it would be a shame, especially as it seems Sandy wanted it to stay in the family.'

'Bel, stop it!' said her sister, giving up on the hints and going for open opposition. 'The poor man has only just arrived. And his decisions are nothing to do with you.'

'I was just asking,' said the child, her blue eyes wide and innocent. 'Now Iain has finally got here and had the chance to look around.'

'I'm here for a week this time,' said Iain, surprised to find he was pleased he hadn't just come for a couple of days. 'As I said before, I knew hardly anything about this place until I arrived. I'll get my bearings, then I'll see.'

'It's strange Sandy left the place to you and not to your father, isn't it?' said Bel.

Iain flinched. That had been a shock, and was still a sore point in the family. Not only had Great-uncle Alex excluded Iain's father from his will, he had also missed his older brother, Stephen. It was very strange.

'Who knows what Great-uncle Alexander's reasons were,' he said.

'But don't you wonder?' asked Bel. 'And what does your father think?'

Before Iain could protest that this was really a bit too intrusive, Lally said, 'Ignore her.' She shook her head in despair. 'She's incurably nosy. The best thing to do is not answer her questions.'

'Of course, if you did want to sell,' continued Bel blithely, 'we know someone who'd be interested in buying. That is to say, someone who might be if we put it to them the right way.'

Iain followed her gaze around to the older sister and saw to his surprise that she was now looking angry rather than uncomfortable. 'Bel, I said stop it.'

Was that what this was all about? Who was Bel talking about? Iain couldn't imagine anyone wanting to spend more than a few weeks in that isolated spot, magnificent views or not.

He was also a little put out. This was his place, as he'd already had to point out forcibly to his family. He didn't like to think that anyone else had designs on it. Oddly disturbed, he decided it was time to take himself off home.

Bel Reveals Her Plans

The following morning Lally rose early to do the first feed of the lambs. The light was pale and fresh and lit the sea brightly and the islands and the mountains on the far shore in a soft haze. Beautiful, all of it. She wasn't sure she'd ever seen it quite like this before, and she had looked on this vista thousands of times. She wondered if their new neighbour was looking at it and appreciating it as he should.

But she had other things to think about today. She had finally arranged a meeting with the Village Hall Committee. She wasn't sure they were quite the right people to approve her plans for promoting an interest in local history, but Gran had said it was the best place to start, and Gran usually knew about these things. It was a shame Gran wasn't here to support her. As chair of the group, and one of the longest-serving and hardest-working members, her words would have carried weight. Not that Lally couldn't manage perfectly well on her own, of course.

Bel was up by the time she had finished with the lambs, busily stirring something on the Rayburn.

'I've made porridge, just like Gran would have done,' she said happily. 'It's nearly ready.'

'But I don't like porridge!' Being able to choose her own breakfast had been one of the few positives of Gran being away.

'I know. But Gran says a decent breakfast will set you up fine for the day, and actually I've been missing it myself.'

'You have it all, then.'

'Don't be like that. There's cream and sugar, you'll love it.'

Lal grunted, but didn't bother to continue the argument. 'Why are you up so early? You know the doctor said you should sleep as long as you could, rest is the best cure for you.'

'I'm fine now. And I can't sleep past eight no matter how hard I try.'

Really, Bel was the most unusual teenager.

'If you're feeling so well maybe we should think of you going back to Glasgow and going back to school for the last few weeks of term? I'm shocked you want to miss out on your studies.'

Bel shrugged and looked away. 'I asked for some books to bring away and I've read them all. I'll be fine.'

She brought the porridge over to the little kitchen table and began to spoon it into the bowls she had laid ready. Lal said no more about school. Secretly she didn't think Bel was quite over the repercussions of the glandular fever. Also, she had no doubt that Bel had already covered more than she needed in the way of schoolwork. That was the way she was, bright and interested and so capable it was scary.

She wasn't feeling so fond of Bel half-an-hour later when the child announced she was coming along to the meeting.

'No, you're not,' said Lal quickly. 'I'll have enough to worry about without you being there.'

'But I'll support you,' protested Bel. 'I'll present the opinion of youth, let them know we are interested in history.'

'You're not exactly a representative of the local youth.'

'I wish I was. I'd love to live here permanently. Then I could join the committee myself. That's what they lack, a younger perspective.'

As the youngest current member of the committee was Anka, who was at least fifty, this point was true. However, Lal ignored it and concentrated on the more important issue. 'You can't live here permanently!' she said, horrified. 'Mum would be heartbroken. And what about school?'

'I could go to school here,' said Bel vaguely. 'Isn't there one in Inverloch?'

'I think the nearest high school is Ullapool. Bel, be reasonable. It's nearly an hour's journey each way, far too much travelling when you've been so unwell.'

'It was just an idea,' said Bel, looking mutinous. 'The local children must go somewhere, mustn't they?'

Lal frowned, trying to remember what she knew about the few local youngsters. 'I suppose they must. There aren't actually that many of them around.'

Bel nodded. 'Which is a pity. Sutherland needs young people like me.'

Lal dried the last of the breakfast dishes and put them away with a bang. 'I haven't time to discuss this now.' Hopefully this was a brief enthusiasm of Bel's and the less said about it the better. 'Ishbel is opening the hall for me at ten and I don't want to keep her waiting. And you can't come, I was counting on you watering Gran's tomatoes and the rest of the things in the greenhouse, and then maybe walking down to see if our new neighbour needs help with anything.'

Bel opened her mouth to protest, and then paused. The chance to ferret more information out of poor Iain Cunningham was obviously too tempting to resist.

'OK, but remember you have to report everything back to me. I'm interested, you know.'

*　*　*

Francie Dunmore had risen early enough to feed the lambs herself, but unfortunately she wasn't at home at Tigh na Mara. She was still in her sister's very nice flat in Broughty Ferry, just outside Dundee, and by the looks of things she'd be here for a while yet. Bridget might be two years the younger, but she had never been robust, and her recent 'funny turn' still hadn't been totally explained. There were to be more tests today.

Francie sighed. It wasn't that she minded taking care of Bridget, of course she didn't, and goodness knew she was desperate for her sister to get better, but if she admitted the truth to herself, she was missing home more than she had thought possible. Were Lally and Bel managing the animals? And the garden? Of course they would be, but what if Lal forgot to water the seedlings, or Bel had a setback in her own illness, the child really was prone to doing far too much . . .

She sighed. It was so unlucky that everything should happen at once. And Sandy's nephew still hadn't come to visit Harbour House so who knew what was to happen there.

'Fra-an,' said a faint voice from the master bedroom (en suite, who would have thought it?). 'Francie? Are you awake?'

'Yes, dear, I'm here. Would you like a nice cup of tea? I've already got the kettle on.' Francie wondered if she had made a mistake putting the water on to boil. Maybe if she hadn't, Bridget would have slept a little longer. And then she felt bad for minding the disturbance. Poor Bridget, she hadn't had a happy life, for all her money. Who could begrudge her a little spoiling now?

Francie was kept busy after that, preparing a tasty breakfast for her sister to eat in bed, then running a bath for her. They needed to be at the hospital for midday and it took Bridget so long to do anything. Of course, she wasn't well, but Francie couldn't help remembering that even as a child her sister had seemed able to waste hours on end doing not very much.

The phone rang as she was finishing the breakfast dishes. She dried her hands and hurried to answer it. Perhaps it was Lally, telling her how everything was going.

It wasn't. It was Hamish McDougall, one of her neighbours. Just hearing his lovely singing accent cheered her. Hamish had taken to ringing her a couple of times a week. She wasn't quite sure why, but it was wonderful to have news of home.

After they had exchanged greetings and Francie had ascertained that, as far as Hamish knew, everything was well on the croft, he moved on to the reason for the call.

'Young Lally is coming to speak to the Hall Committee this lunchtime,' he said. 'You mind she arranged it a wee while back?'

'Yes, of course.' Francie kicked herself for letting this slip her memory. Lally had this idea of setting up some local history group and was desperate to see it succeed. She said there was so much to find out about the area. Unfortunately, Francie doubted her enthusiasm would be shared by many of her neighbours. 'You'll go and support her, won't you?'

'Aye, I'll go along and have a wee listen. But I thought you should know, Margery is very against the idea, and Anka thinks we're spreading our efforts too thinly as it is. I cannae think she's going to persuade them.'

'It's not as though it would take much of their time,' said Francie. She sighed. They'd been over these points before. She wished Lally had waited until she was back before she faced the committee. But the way things were going, she could have wasted the whole summer by then, and Lal, like all the Dunmores, liked to act once she had an idea.

'The way the lassie is talking, it'll take all of our time and more besides. Arranging digs, trips to Edinburgh to see the archives, mounting a permanent display in the hall.'

Oh dear, thought Francie. Lal's ideas had obviously moved on since she had last heard them. 'Perhaps you could persuade her to try one thing at a time, to begin with at least.'

'Aye, that's what I thought. She should start with the meetings.'

Francie was surprised and pleased. 'So you don't think the history society is a bad idea? I'm glad.'

'I think it'll be a fine thing.'

38

'I hope so. Lal is keen, I'd hate her to be disappointed. And I've just thought, if you can find a role for Margery in the society or whatever it is, that might make her more positive.'

'Aye, you're right there. Maybe I'll drop the idea into the conversation.'

After the phone call Francie was left more confused and worried than before it. From what Hamish had said, Lally was bursting with enthusiasm about her new project, which was a good thing, wasn't it? But if she upset Margery and Anka and, heaven forbid, Ishbel, it could take Francie months to soothe their ruffled feathers. And then it seemed Hamish was interested in this history stuff. Why had she never realised that before? And now he was actually taking the initiative and saying he would help involve Margery.

Possibly more worrying, why on earth did he keep phoning her? No-one in their wildest dreams could have called Hamish McDougall the chatty type.

She was brought back to the present by her sister calling for help to get out of the bath. She put thoughts of Strathan aside, and hurried to assist, pointing out that the water really hadn't got that cold, and they would be in plenty of time for the hospital if Bridget would only decide which of her many outfits to wear today.

'Who Has The Time For This?'

Iain had slept better than he had expected in the strange bed. He wasn't sure he would like being up on the sleeping platform, with the steep wooden ceiling stretching above him, but he had fallen asleep almost at once and when he had woken the sunlight was streaming in through the Velux windows.

He made himself tea and toast for breakfast, feeling thankful he had thought to bring at least basic food supplies with him. There didn't seem to be any shops for miles. Then he took out his laptop and mobile and set out to see what kind of connection he could get here.

To his surprise and relief, it wasn't too bad. He'd realised yesterday that mobile reception was reasonable, and he managed to connect the phone to the laptop and hook into his e-mails with no bother at all. Excellent. This made him look on the place in a much better light. If he could access the internet then he wouldn't feel so isolated.

He had meant to spend the morning exploring the property, but one thing led to another, the way it did with e-mails and work, and a couple of hours had passed when he heard a knock on the door.

He frowned. Maybe he had been a little too friendly to the neighbours last night. He really didn't want them dropping in on him at all times of day.

It was the youngster, Bel. She had let herself in before he had even risen from his seat.

'Morning, morning, how are you? Have you looked around yet? Oops, this is Pup, do you mind if he comes in?'

'Looks like he already is in,' said Iain, eyeing the dog. It was some kind of collie, not that he knew much about dogs.

'He's only a pup, which is why we call him Pup, although Lal says if Gran doesn't hurry up and name him soon he won't answer to anything else. Gran got him to help with the sheep, but he's the world's worst sheepdog. He's scared of other animals, would you believe it? And he doesn't like being left alone, either, he whines like anything, which is why I brought him with me.'

'I remember him from last night. He seems friendly enough.'

'He's lovely, although not much use as a guard dog. Not that you need a guard dog round here.'

Iain put a hand down to the dog which rubbed up against him in a friendly way. It was a nice enough animal, with soft silky fur.

'Can I offer you a drink?' he asked the girl, feeling he should be hospitable now she was here. The Dunmores had fed him last night, after all.

'No, thanks. Have you looked around yet? I thought I could show you a couple of things, then I need to get

43

back to hang the washing out.'

Iain was glad to hear that she wouldn't be spending the whole day with him.

'Is your sister not around?'

'No, she's off to board the Hall Committee. I wanted to go with her but . . . ' Bel paused, for once interrupting herself mid-flow. 'Wow, have you got your laptop working here? Are you connected to the internet?' She slid on to the seat beside him and stared avidly at the screen.

Iain couldn't help feeling flattered by her interest. 'Yes, via my mobile here. I see there is a phone line, but it isn't connected at the moment and I'm not sure there'll be broadband here.'

'There isn't,' said Bel, her tone disgusted. 'It's ridiculous, they're supposed to be supporting remote and rural communities, but when we ask for something as basic as that they say there's no demand. Of course there's no demand at the moment, because nobody realises what it can do for them!'

Iain supposed this was true. He

hadn't really thought of broadband from the point of view of the locals, he just wanted it for his own benefit.

'Can you show me how it works with a mobile? I wonder if I can get something set up like this?'

He spent the next half hour showing the child his computer and explaining how she could set up something similar herself, if she had access to the right technology. She seemed fascinated, asking for explanations of anything she didn't understand and listening carefully. It was rather nice finding someone who was happy to let him talk about Information Technology. Of course, he talked to people at his work, but this was different. He felt like he was making a convert, and he was enjoying it.

Eventually Bel remembered why she had come down here. She nudged Pup off her feet and stood up. 'I'd better get back. If you don't hang out the washing earlyish in the day there's no chance of it drying, even in this weather. And we always have masses of washing. Gran looks after a couple of holiday cottages so it can be never ending. Do you want me to show you where Sandy kept everything or are you OK on your own? Don't worry, just tell me if I'm interfering.'

Iain smiled. He couldn't imagine this child not interfering, but he was feeling kindly to her now so he accepted her offer and followed her outside.

Despite the sunny day the ground was still wet from the dew, or maybe it had rained in the night. Iain suspected that the ground around here was wet a lot, maybe most of the time.

As Bel showed him round, he realised there was a kind of logic to the buildings. The house itself, with its broad doorway and windows to right and left, with two dormers above (but no roof) stood four-square to the sea. It had an ideal view of the jetty — even at his most optimistic Iain wouldn't have called this bay a harbour.

At right angles to the house, and

further away from the jetty, was the Bothy. Behind this were the buildings which Bel explained had been used for the farming side of the business. As Bel had warned him the previous day, the hay barn only had half an upper floor, so you had to be wary where you walked.

'So Harbour House was a farm? I thought it was something to do with the, er, harbour and fishing.'

'I think the original occupant was the Harbour Master, but they would have farmed, too. People round here put their hand to all kinds of work, always have. I think Harbour House once had quite a big holding of land, but that has all been let elsewhere now. Sandy just had the buildings and this bit of garden. See how the space in front is sheltered? He'd started planting it out until he got ill a couple of years ago. He said he was impressed with everything Gran managed to grow and was going to see what he could do himself. It's all weeds now, but it wouldn't take much to sort it out.'

'I'm not much of a gardener,' said Iain quickly. 'Why did Great-uncle Alex — Sandy — renovate the Bothy and not the house?'

'He was planning to do the house next. The Bothy took longer than he expected. Gran said it was because he was such a perfectionist, but you have to admit he did a good job. That was for him to live in. He was going to do up the house to take paying guests, either as bed and breakfast or self-catering. There's a lot of demand for that round here. And after he'd done the house he was going to start on the outbuildings. That barn would make a nice wee cottage.'

Iain murmured non-commitally. With the drooping corrugated-iron roofs and collapsing walls he personally thought it would be easier to demolish the outbuildings and start from scratch. He had to admit, though, the house did have potential. The walls had been recently repaired and Bel pointed out to him where places had been made for the rafters to sit. 'Sandy had even ordered them, I think they're still sitting at the builder's yard in Inverloch. He was keen to continue with his plans, even after the second heart attack. Gran tried to get him to slow down but Sandy wasn't like that.' Bel sighed heavily.

Iain felt a moment of guilt. How was it he hadn't known his great uncle, and these people had? And, from the sound of it, had done their best to look after him.

'Do you have any pictures of him?' he asked, surprising himself. 'I'd like to know what he looked like.' And to know more about him, he realised, but he didn't say that.

'Yes, probably. Why don't you come up later on when Lal is back? She can look them out for you. Now I must get back to that washing.'

And she hurried back up the hill to the little white house, sounding like a busy housewife although she still looked like a waif.

Lally had laid out her display with great care. She had persuaded Ishbel to help her move one of the big tables into the middle of the hall. In the centre of this she put a map of the area, with places of known historical interest marked in red. Bel had helped by drawing pictures to identify each one — the broch at Sandness, the souterrain close to Hamish's croft, the possible burial cairn beyond where the Urig and Meallan rivers met.

Then there were her finds. The few pieces of pottery, the Victorian coins, bones from the cave on the shore. None of these were of earth-shattering interest. Lally didn't mind that. It was the day-to-day details of how people had lived in earlier times that fascinated her. She suspected, however, that people would take her idea of a local history group — and museum — more seriously if she had a really big find to show them.

She was so busy trying to present all this to best advantage she was shocked to hear the outer door open once again. She glanced at her watch. It was midday already.

Ishbel reappeared, tall and gaunt. 'Is no-one here yet? It's always the same. Honestly, I don't know why people can't be on time.'

'I'm running a bit late myself,' admitted Lally. 'I'll just switch the kettle on and bring the sandwiches through.'

'I really don't think it was necessary to promise everyone lunch, it's not as though they can't feed themselves. I hope they're not going to expect something like this at every meeting.'

'I'm sure they won't,' said Lally soothingly. 'You don't normally meet at lunchtime, do you? I thought I should reward everyone for coming out in the middle of the day like this.'

Ishbel pressed her thin lips together and looked unconvinced.

Fortunately Hamish arrived at that

point. He went straight over to the big table and began to look at the display. 'Well, haven't you done us proud?'

'Looks like something you might expect from a primary school class,' said Ishbel, before Lally could get ideas above her station. She supposed Ishbel would know, being a retired primary school teacher herself. Lally often wondered why the local families spoke so glowingly of the old woman, she would have thought being taught by her was enough to destroy any enthusiasm you had for life.

By the time she had brought through the industrial-sized pot of tea and plates for the sandwiches, the last two members of the Hall Management Committee had arrived. Margery, well-dressed and with far too much make up for the occasion, and Anka, who looked like she had come straight from milking her goats, and probably had.

Strictly speaking the committee did have other members, but as they rarely attended and never spoke out, Lally knew it was these four she needed to convince.

She made sure they all had something to eat and drink and answered their questions about the new arrival at Harbour House. 'I believe he's here for a few days this time, no, I don't know when he'll be back, yes, he seems very pleasant.' Then she moved on to what she really wanted to talk about: her proposal. They all had some idea of what it was about, she'd had to give a reason for the meeting, but now she needed to flesh it out, get their support.

She had twin aims. One was to awaken an interest in the fascinating local history among the community, from the youngest to the oldest. People should know about their past, what had come before them in the world. And there was far more to the history of this area than just the story of the clearances.

Her second aim was to find somewhere to display the information and finds, and use this as an attraction to bring in more tourists. She was sure this would encourage visitors to stay longer in the area, and spend more money whilst they were here. The village hall would be the initial base, but in the long run they should aim for a purpose-built museum. Perhaps they could manage a shop and café as well! That would be wonderful. She could see it all before her, and forgot to be shy as she tried to explain her vision to the others.

They let her speak to the end, either too nonplussed by it all, or more interested in the sandwiches she and Bel had prepared.

'Well,' she said when she had eventually run down. 'What do you think?' She was starting to wish she had let Bel come along. At least there would have been one supporting voice.

'It's very ambitious,' said Ishbel. 'And I don't like to be discouraging, but really who has the time for this?'

'And where would we get the money?' said Anka, her Norwegian accent still strong despite the decades she had lived in Scotland.

'I think it's a fine idea,' said Hamish, his own accent reminiscent of the Gaelic which was his mother tongue.

'I've never been very interested in history,' said Margery, and Lally's heart sank. Margery's accent was as pure middle-England as Hamish's was Highland. She and her husband, a keen fisherman, had retired to the area a couple of years ago. Margery had time on her hands and support from her would have been a real boost. She pursed her painted lips. 'However, the way you explain it all, it actually seems quite fascinating.'

Hamish jumped in before anyone else could speak. 'Aye, it sounds fascinating all right. And I think we could learn from the interest newcomers like yourself, Margery, take in everything about the area. It's a fine example to the local folk that you're so keen.'

Margery tried to look modest and Ishbel frowned. 'Local people are busy,' she said dourly. 'The idea might be appealing, of course, but we have to be realistic. We struggle to find anyone to help with basic things like the hall cleaning rota. How are we going to get people to volunteer for this?'

'It will have to be us, as usual,' said Anka. 'And I do not have the time.'

'No, it doesn't have to be you,' said Lally. 'My plan is to get a wide range of people interested, and if they're interested they'll be happy to give up their time. I need your support, but I'm more than happy to do the initial organising.'

'That's very kind of you, but you don't live here all year round,' said Ishbel. 'Who will take over when you go back to Edinburgh? And don't say your grandmother, because goodness knows she already has enough on her plate.'

Lal hesitated. She couldn't tell them that what she really wanted was to move permanently to the area. She hadn't even told her own family that. They would be as appalled at that idea as they would be at Bel wishing to stay. And, realistically, Lal wouldn't have the money to do it for a few years. Maybe she was being precipitate, talking to them about her ideas now.

'I think we should give it a try,' said Hamish in his slow way. Lally flashed him a grateful smile. He was being far more supportive than she had expected.

'I agree,' said Margery, still preening from Hamish's words. 'I've been saying for a while, we need to be more forward-looking, willing to try something new.'

'A historical society is not, I think, forward looking,' said Anka.

Lal hadn't actually thought of her plans in terms of a Historical Society, but she quite liked the sound of that.

'Let's think it over and consider it at our next full meeting,' said Ishbel. 'Maybe Francie will be back by then and we can hear her thoughts.'

'She likes the idea,' said Lally, but then felt guilty. Was Gran just supporting her because she was family? 'But I don't want it to be more work for her. As you say, she has enough to do.'

'It might be a wee while yet before Francie returns,' said Hamish. 'Why don't we make a start in the meantime? Nothing lost if Lally arranges a first meeting of the Historical Society, is there? And maybe Margery could help her, it would be good to have someone to take an organising role.'

'It certainly would,' agreed Lal, who knew organisation wasn't her strong point. She would never have thought of asking Margery, but the woman was now positively beaming.

'Well, I'd be only too happy to help, if you think I could be useful. I think we should have a first meeting soon, I'm dying to hear more.'

Hamish nodded encouragingly. 'There you go then, Lally. You and Margery go ahead and set something up. I'd like fine to know more about the history of the area myself.'

'You know lots already,' said Lal, smiling gratefully at him. 'It would be brilliant if you were involved.' She would actually have preferred his help to Margery's, but she knew how busy he was on his croft.

'Go ahead if you think you can manage it,' said Anka. 'But don't count on me. And now I need to be home.'

The meeting broke up soon after. Ishbel stayed to help Lally wash the cups and plates and clear away her displays.

'I see you've gone to a lot of trouble,' she said. Lal wasn't sure if this indicated approval or the opposite.

'Not really,' she said.

She needed to decide what to do next. Margery had already promised to phone and arrange to come round to Tigh na Mara for a chat. They could get Bel to draw some posters and see if she could rally support for a first meeting.

The Strathan Historical Society, Margery had called it. And once that was up and running and everyone saw how fascinating the subject was, she would work some more on the idea of a local museum. She could picture it already. A smallish building, very environmentally friendly, with perhaps a reconstructed black house beside it. Now that was an excellent idea . . .

'Right, that's us finished,' said Ishbel, rousing her from these happy thoughts. 'Off you go. I'll lock up, then I'll know it's been done properly.'

Learning About The Past

'So were they keen?' demanded Bel as soon as she got home. 'Are they going to support you?'

Lally shrugged uncomfortably. 'I don't really know. At first there wasn't much enthusiasm, apart from Hamish. Amazing to hear him being positive. And then Margery started being quite helpful. I think she sees a role for herself as chairperson, or secretary at the very least.'

'Great. You'll need all the help you can get.'

'Yes. I will. Now, can you help me carry all this stuff back into the house?'

They stowed the materials in the cupboard in Lally's room and then it was time to feed the lambs once again. Bel had already made up the milk and they went out together. It was easier if there were two of them, and Lally had

61

long since given up trying to get her sister to continue with her afternoon nap.

'I went down to see Iain,' said Bel, catching up the smallest lamb and settling with it between her legs. 'You'll never believe it, he's got an Internet connection!'

'How come? The phone in the Bothy isn't even working according to Gran.'

'Via his mobile. It's brilliant, Lal. It shows you can get technology to work out here. And it's given me an idea. What do you think of this — I could live here with Gran and be home-schooled. I wouldn't need to travel anywhere.' The child grinned in delight. 'With the Internet you can get hold of any information you need these days. It would be brilliant!'

'Bel, I really don't think this is a good idea . . . '

'You're moving out here. Why shouldn't I?'

'Who said I was moving out here? At the moment I'm house-sitting whilst Gran is away.'

'But I know you want to. That's why you were so interested in Harbour House, wasn't it?'

'As if I could afford to buy Harbour House,' said Lal, not answering the question. She had saved a little, very little, money from her year's working at the museum. It was nowhere near enough to buy a property and she had no steady income to allow her to get a mortgage. But that didn't stop her yearning to live at Strathan all year round. Bel was right. This was what Lally wanted, had wanted for years. She just had to find a way of making it happen.

'Something will probably turn up,' said Bel and Lal smiled as she recognised one of her own favourite phrases. 'You'll have to stay here if you want the local historical thing to get off the ground. And you know you can live with Gran as long as you like.'

'So you and I are going to move in here long term, are we?' Lal shook her head. 'There's really not much room. It's fine while Gran's away and I can use her bedroom but once she's home and we're back to sharing . . . No, I can't see that working for long.'

Bel was unbearably tidy. The two girls hadn't shared a room at home in Glasgow for years and Lal really didn't want to go back to that now.

'I was thinking about moving into that box room under the eaves,' said Bel. 'We could fit a bed and a little table in there, I wouldn't need anything more.' She released one lamb and nimbly caught up another.

'It's minute, and damp, and full of spiders.'

'It can be cleaned, you know.'

'I think it needs a new window, too. Didn't Gran say the window was so rotten she hardly dared touch it?'

'It'll be a good reason to get her to replace it. I'll suggest it to her.'

'Bel! I really don't think Mum and Dad are going to agree to this.'

'They wouldn't object to you moving here.'

Lal wasn't so sure about that,

actually. Her father had high hopes of her pursuing an academic career, as he himself had done. 'I'm twenty-three. I can make up my own mind. You're only fourteen.'

'I'll talk them round,' said Bel confidently. 'It would make them visit more often, which would be a good thing. Dad loves it, when he makes the effort to get here. I wonder if he'd like to move back when he eventually retires?'

'Mum would never agree.'

'True. Too far from Marks and Spencers.'

The two sisters exchanged knowing smiles. Lal was beginning to feel cheered by this conversation, although she didn't know why. Bel was so incurably positive it was hard not to start believing there must be a way to get things to 'work out'.

Towards the end of the afternoon Iain walked the short distance to Tigh na Mara. He had said to Bel he would call in and he was keen to see some photographs of his Great Uncle Alex, but it still felt unnatural to be going to visit like this. He hardly knew these people and here he was about to meet them (well, Bel) for the fifth time in two days. Surely they would think he was imposing?

He was about to knock on the solid front door when the older sister, Lally, came around the side of the building. Her thick hair was blowing loose from its clip and she pushed it back with one hand and gave him a broad smile. 'Hello there! You're just in time for a cup of tea. Bel said to expect you. Come round the side here, I've got the conservatory door open, you have to make the most of this good weather.'

Iain wouldn't actually have said the weather was good — sunny, yes, but rather cool and windy — but he didn't disagree. He followed her around to where the wide conservatory doors were clipped back. The view from here really was lovely, better, even, than from Harbour House. This place was slightly higher so you could see right across the blue-grey water of the bay to the mountains that rose in curtain after curtain beyond.

'I believe Bel has been baking scones, so I hope you're feeling hungry,' continued Lally, ushering him inside. Once they were indoors she took the slide from her hair and rearranged it into a fairly tidy pony tail. Iain found himself watching her. He'd never seen anyone with hair quite like that, so long and wild.

'I hope Bel hasn't gone to any bother for me,' he said.

'She likes baking. She was glad of the excuse. And I thought it was better for her to do that than begin making up the lazy beds, which was her other plan.'

'Lazy beds?' said Iain, confused.

'Yes. You know, the way of digging seaweed into the soil to make it more fertile? It's been done in this area for centuries. Believe me, lazy beds is a definite misnomer, they are very hard work. I'm trying to get Bel to take things easy.'

Iain couldn't prevent himself smiling. 'I bet that's a challenge.'

'It is. Have a seat and I'll go and see how she's doing.'

A few moments later the two girls returned. Bel was carrying a tray with all the paraphernalia for an old-fashioned tea; milk in a jug, sugar in a pot and a little silver tea strainer.

Lally had a plate of scones in one hand and a large photo album in the other. She put them down on the cane and glass table and collapsed into a seat beside him.

'Phew, I'm glad to sit down!'

'That's because you've been doing the lazy beds,' said Bel disapprovingly. 'Don't deny it because I saw you. You should have let me help.'

'Maybe tomorrow,' said Lally. She turned to pass a cup and saucer to Iain. 'Bel said you'd like to see some pictures of Sandy so I brought the album through. We can have a look after we've eaten.'

Iain took one of the scones that Bel

was offering and complimented her on her baking. He couldn't remember when he had last had home-made scones.

'It's Gran's secret recipe,' said Bel with a giggle, showing her metal-clad teeth.

Iain found himself smiling back at her. She was such a bright little thing.

'Did you know my uncle well?' he asked, thinking of the man who was a stranger to him.

It was Lal who answered. 'Gran knew him best, but we all saw him whenever we visited. He got along really well with Gramps from the day he bought the place, that must be about ten years ago, and he was often up at the house here.'

'Gran likes having people to cook for,' said Bel.

'And Gramps liked a bit of DIY. I have to say, sometimes I think he'd rather have been a builder than a crofter. If Sandy wasn't up here, Gramps was down there helping out with this and that.'

'Or talking to him while Sandy did the hard work,' said Bel.

'Well, specially after his stroke, he couldn't do much lifting and so on, and he did like the company,' said Lal. 'And as Gramps got more ill, Sandy was a great help to Gran. Lots of people were, of course, because that's how it works round here, but Sandy was particularly good. I know Gran said she didn't think Gramps could have stayed at home in the end if Sandy hadn't been here to help her lift him and so on.'

Iain tried to match this picture of the supportive neighbour with the one he had from his father, of the maverick who always did what he wanted and cared nothing for the family. 'I wish I'd known him,' he said.

Lal shot him a curious look, but it was Bel who said, 'Why didn't you ever come and visit?' Even on so short an acquaintance Iain had realised tact was not Bel's strong point.

Iain shrugged. 'We weren't really in touch. In fact, I think Great Uncle Alex had retired and moved up here a couple of years before we even heard about it.'

'I wonder why he chose to leave everything to you.'

'Bel!' said her sister warningly.

'I just wondered. Iain has an older brother, don't you? And yet Sandy left it all to you, not him.'

'I certainly never expected it,' said Iain. He felt like he was being accused. For the first time he wondered who these people had expected to inherit. If his uncle had been as close to the girls' gran as it seemed, did they think she should have got Harbour House? But that was ridiculous. Friends were one thing, but family was quite another.

'Here, I'll show you some photos,' said Lally calmly, reaching for the album.

It was years since Iain had handled a photo album. He thought that nowadays everyone had digital photos, sending them to each other by e-mail or mobile phone, but clearly not.

This album started when Lally was slightly younger than Bel was now (and looking very like her). The girl skipped over her own family pictures until she came to one of a tall, wiry man with grey hair worn in a crew-cut. 'That's Sandy,' she said. 'That's not long after he moved here. He'd be in his mid-sixties then, very fit and active.'

For a moment Iain said nothing. The man looked uncannily similar to how he remembered his own grandfather; a fitter, out-door version of the successful business man.

'Here's a few of him and Gramps working on the Bothy, you can see what a mess it was to begin with. That's the caravan Sandy lived in for the first few years. Here's him teaching me and Bel to sail. He was a great guy, a real outdoors person. We were all very surprised when he had the heart attack, he always seemed so fit.

'Look, he hasn't even got a wetsuit on although we have and we were still freezing!'

Lal turned the pages, making the occasional comment. Iain got the impression of a generous, friendly man, good with children, fond of a dram or two. Why had he lost contact with his own family? 'Why did he never marry?' he asked, before he could stop himself.

'Oh, I think he did,' said Lal, looking surprised. 'I'm sure Gran said he was married for a while, a long time ago. But it didn't work out, maybe because he was away at sea so much. A shame he didn't have children. He was very good with us.'

Iain found viewing the pictures oddly unsettling. He was glad when they came to the end of the album and he could put it to one side. He had wanted to know more about his uncle, and now he did. Instead of putting everything into perspective, it just seemed to raise more questions. He shook his head, irritated. He liked everything in life to be tidy, to make sense. Maybe that was why he had put off coming up here for so long. It didn't fit with his idea of his family and himself, and he didn't like that.

'Thank you very much for showing

me those,' he said, sounding prim even to himself.

'No problem, you're welcome,' said Lal. 'You can take the album away with you if you want to have another look. Gran won't mind.'

'No, it's all right.'

'You can ask us as many questions as you like,' added Bel. 'And hopefully Gran will be back in a few weeks, you'll want to meet her and see what she remembers of Sandy.'

'I'm only here until Friday,' said Iain repressively. He was just about to make a move to depart when he realised Bel had poured him another cup of tea. He sighed and picked it up to drink as quickly as he could.

'I suppose you've got a long drive to get home,' said Lal. 'You live in London, don't you?'

'London? No, I used to, but now I'm in Edinburgh.'

'Edinburgh's really close,' said Bel disapprovingly. 'I'm sure Sandy didn't know you were there, he would have loved you to visit sooner.'

'I've only just moved there. In fact, I haven't even officially started my new job, which is why I need to get back and get organised.' He wondered why he was taking the trouble to explain.

'I suppose being in Edinburgh made it easier to visit here at long last,' said Lal. Her tone was neutral, but Iain couldn't help feeling he was being judged. It was ridiculous. What did his movements have to do with these girls?

'Lal used to live in Edinburgh,' said Bel, following her own line of thought. 'That's where she studied and worked for a year.'

'Bel! Iain's not interested in that.'

'And now she's going to move back here and open a museum,' continued Bel, grinning. 'She'll be the official historian for the area.'

Iain presumed this was a joke. 'Of course an area like this wouldn't have call for a resident historian,' he said. 'Or a museum. Goodness, who would there be to visit it?'

Lal's expression, so far either friendly or neutral, suddenly became stormy.

'People only say things like that because they don't know what they're talking about,' she said, putting down her mug with a bang. 'There is as much demand to know about the past here as anywhere. People want to understand where they're from. Why shouldn't Strathan have a museum? And it wouldn't just be for the locals, it would draw people in.'

'That's right,' said Bel loyally. 'It's going to be brilliant. We just need to persuade everyone else of that. And find funding.'

Lal sighed, the fight going out of her. 'Yes, well, let's not bore Iain with that now. Would you like any more tea? I can refill the pot.'

'No, no, time I was on my way.'

Iain left soon after, with the distinct feeling he had ruffled Lal's feathers. In a way he was pleased. At least he wasn't the only one left unsettled by the afternoon's conversation.

An Opportunity Arises

Iain was determined to see as little of the girls as possible during the rest of his stay. What he needed to do was familiarise himself with Harbour House and decide whether or not to put it on the market. Actually, make that decide when to put it on the market. This had been Great Uncle Alex's dream, not his. He had a life in Edinburgh to build for himself.

He busied himself exploring the derelict buildings and walking the shoreline. One day he drove into Inverloch. It was time he got a feel for the place, and he was badly in need of food supplies. He even visited the builders' yard where he had been told some of Great Uncle Alex's orders were still sitting waiting for collection, paid for months ago.

He introduced himself to a thickset, chatty man who he took to be the owner, Jimmy Jones. The man seemed to have all the time in the world and was keen to know when Iain had arrived, what he thought of the area, and Harbour House, and so on and so on. Iain really couldn't get used to how people around here liked to talk.

He was even more amazed when he saw the supplies that awaited him. There were roofing joists, and planks of wood the man called sarking, and rows and rows of slates. And metres of cast-iron guttering. And heavy wooden window frames. In fact, there appeared to be the wherewithal to turn Harbour House from its current ruined state to something like a proper house.

'He'd ordered all this?' he said, looking at it blankly.

'Aye,' said the owner in his slow way. 'Been sitting here for nigh on eight months, so it has. When do you want me to deliver it?'

'Deliver? Well, I'm not here for long just now and I'd have to find a roofer . . . ' Iain trailed off. What was he doing, talking about a roofer? He was about to sell the place.

'You'll no be doing the work yourself?'

'No!' The idea of clambering around at height made Iain feel quite ill.

'I can recommend a couple of guys might take the job on for you, if you'd like. I'd stay clear of Billy from Strathan, if I was you. He means well but never finishes a job. It's the McMichaels you want. They're probably busy the now, with it being such good weather, but you can talk to them and see.'

'That's very kind of you,' said Iain, and found himself taking note of the builder's name and phone number. He felt he was being rushed, and he had never liked that. He didn't have to phone them immediately, did he? He arranged for the various things to continue to be stored in the builder's yard for the time being, apologised for taking up space like that, then made his escape.

And yet he couldn't help thinking, as

he drove carefully along the winding road back to Harbour House, that maybe the place would sell better if he did get the roof put on. It would be a shame not to, with all the supplies already on hand. It only need delay putting it on the market for a few months, surely.

He was thinking these thoughts as he rounded the corner to Strathan Bay. He slowed to take in the view of the cliffs with their natural stone arch, and the scattered houses of the village, and Harbour House itself. He knew you weren't supposed to park in the passing places but he drew into one for a minute so he could take it all in. Just looking on this place made him feel calmer.

Someone was working with a tractor in one of the higher fields, and two boys in wet suits were body-surfing in the bay. Apart from that it was just the sound of the waves and the birds calling over-head. He wound down his window and breathed in the salty scent of the shore.

'Hello there!' said a cheery voice, making him jump.

The youngster, Bel, had appeared beside him on a bike. 'I've just cycled over to Drummore for milk,' she explained, pink-faced.

'I've been into Inverloch myself, I could have picked some up for you.' Iain felt guilty. He hadn't even thought of offering to shop for them, but it would have been the neighbourly thing to do. It was a twenty mile round trip to the bigger town and he thought it was at least four miles to the tiny shop at Drummore. He eyed the girl with respect. 'That's quite some cycle ride just for milk.'

'It's good for me,' she said, grinning. 'I'm trying to get fit again. Lally wanted to take the car but I promised not to go too fast. It was fine.' She leant forward to rest her arm on the handle bars. 'And how have you been doing? I wanted to come down and see you, but Lally said we should leave you in peace. You do know you only need to ask if

81

there's anything you want to find out? Or I could take you a walk out to the point, show you the archway, and . . . '

'That's very kind of you,' said Iain quickly, remembering it was generally a good idea to cut Bel off before she got in to full flow.

'No problem, I'd enjoy it. It would be good for you to get to know the place. We could . . . '

'Can you do proper surfing here?' asked Iain. He had just realised the boys weren't body-surfing, they had boards and one of them was now trying (and failing) to stand on his.

Bel followed his gaze and frowned slightly. 'Our bay's not usually popular, I don't see why they had to come here. But there are places nearby that are supposed to be excellent. You can hire kit and get lessons if you're interested.'

'I don't think it's quite my kind of thing. What about you?'

She shrugged. 'Maybe I'll try it. It's never seemed worthwhile when we were only here for holidays, but if I'm going to live here I'd quite like to give it a go.'

Iain wondered if there was anything this bright little girl wasn't interested in.

'Why don't you ask those youngsters if you can join them?' Iain was impressed to see that the more adventurous one was now managing to stand on his board for at least five seconds. 'They look like they're having fun.'

'Oh, no.' Bel's voice immediately lost its jolly tone and she seemed to withdraw into herself. 'I couldn't just go and talk to them. In fact, I'd best get home, Lally will wonder where I've been.'

She raised a hand in a wave and continued down the hill. Iain watched her with a frown. Something hadn't been quite right there. For the first time since he'd met her, Bel had looked worried. He turned back to the boys, wondering if they were local and Bel had some problem with them.

He decided to park the car at the edge of the bay and go over and have a better look himself. He'd thought surfing was something you could do in Cornwall or California. Not Scotland!

He wandered down to the shoreline and exchanged a few words with the boys, who seemed pleasant enough. It seemed odder than ever that he was willing to chat to them and Bel, normally so friendly, had hurried away. Still, it was nothing to do with him. He should be thinking about what needed doing in the next day or so at Harbour House, and then heading back to his real life in Edinburgh.

★ ★ ★

Lally was surprised how much she noticed Iain Cunningham's absence. He'd only been here for a week so there was no reason to miss him. Especially as he hadn't even come up to say goodbye, which would have been the friendly thing to do.

She decided just to forget all about him and concentrate on keeping up to speed with the many jobs around Tigh na Mara, not to mention arranging the first meeting of the Strathan Historical Society. It was so lovely to be in the Highlands at this time of year. The days were long and sunny, if not always warm. Apart from the niggling worry about what the future held for her (and Bel), most of the time she could just enjoy being there.

Unexpectedly, a possible plan for the future was presented to her a week or so after Iain's departure. It wasn't what Lally had expected or hoped for, but she felt she had to give it some consideration. It started with a phone call from Mike Herriot, one of her old university lecturers.

'I got this number from your mother, I hope you don't mind me calling?'

'Of course not. How are you doing?' Lal was surprised to hear from him, but far too polite to say so. True, Mike had been instrumental in getting her the post at the museum, and they had gone out for drink once or twice since then, but they weren't exactly close.

They chatted about general things for a while and then he asked, 'Are you planning to stay in Sutherland for long?'

'I'm not really sure. I'm house-sitting for my gran and I don't know yet when she'll be back.'

'Ah. There's something I wanted to show you. The Department are thinking of taking on a tutor-assistant next year and we thought you might be interested.'

A job in the History Department at the university! Lal wondered why she didn't feel more excited. It would be the chance to work in the field she loved so much, and build up a little money for the eventual move to Strathan. The only problem was, it would take her away from Strathan in the meantime.

'Gosh, that sounds interesting,' she said. She had to show she appreciated him letting her know. 'When would it start? I need to stay here for a while. And of course you'd have to advertise, there's no guarantee I would get it . . .'

'Of course not, we'll have to go through the proper channels. But I discussed it with the Prof and we both felt we should let you know, make sure you looked out for the advert. It'll be in the newspaper next week, but if you were in town I could have shown you a copy of the job specification. I don't suppose you'll be popping back to Edinburgh any time soon?'

'No. I can't leave the croft until Gran comes home.' Lally hesitated. The more she thought about it, the more this job sounded ideal. She would certainly like to know more details, but she didn't want to be presumptuous. 'I know it's a lot to ask, but could you post the information to me?'

'I suppose I could.' Mike sounded reluctant and she immediately felt bad. It was really good of him to think of her like this, she shouldn't expect anything more.

She said quickly, 'No, no I don't want to put you to any trouble. I'll look out for the advert in the paper and then go through the proper channels.'

'It's no problem, I'll send it on. I

thought it'd be rather nice to meet up for a drink, but that will have to wait. Hang on while I get a pen and you can give me your address.'

After the call had ended Lally dashed off to give the news to Bel, and then wished she hadn't. Bel, of course, thought Lal getting the job was a foregone conclusion, which it definitely wasn't. Working hard at being sensible and trying to get Bel to put her ideas into perspective was good for Lal, it made her realise how unlikely this was actually to happen. This, of course, only made her realise what a great job it would be if she did get it, despite it meaning a move back to Edinburgh.

* * *

Lal and Bel's parents were due to visit in a couple of weeks' time, and Lal was beginning to worry. Bel was still being rather strange about returning to Glasgow.

'It'll be great for you to see them,' she

said to her sister. 'Maybe you could even go back home with them afterwards.'

'Lal, I told you, I'm not going back to Glasgow.'

'You'll need to go back in time for the new school year.'

Bel looked sullen. 'No I won't.'

'You can't be serious about this home schooling?' Lal shook her head. 'You'll be lonely. You'll miss meeting and learning with other kids.'

'I will not,' said Bel, looking away this time as though unable to meet her sister's eyes. 'I won't miss the people at that school at all. I never want to see them again.'

There was a moments silence as Lal took in the depth of anger in her sister's voice.

'Oh,' she said. 'Oh.' She felt as though she had been slapped. Bel was totally serious. Bel didn't just dislike the school, she hated it. When had that happened? Why hadn't any of them realised?

'It can't really have been that bad,' she asked, sounding feeble even to herself. 'I quite enjoyed my time there.'

'You had friends,' said Bel bluntly.

Lally frowned, trying to work out where all this had come from. If anyone had asked, she would have said her little sister was popular and happy, always in the thick of things, fascinated by everything, able to talk to adults just as easily as children. She'd certainly been like that when she was at primary school.

Then she had moved to the senior school where Lally and Ant had gone, and had seemed more subdued. Lal wished she had paid more attention to what was happening at that time, but she was already away at university in Edinburgh. She recalled that Bel's good friend, Katy, had moved down to England a year or so ago. And then what?

'Are you being . . . bullied?' she asked, appalled. Surely her parents would have noticed? They both worked in education, her father as a lecturer and her mother as a teacher. 'You should have said!'

'They'll just say it isn't bullying.'

'But what has been happening, Bel? If you tell us we can do something to help.' Lally put out her hand to touch her sister, wanting to understand and give comfort.

Bel shrugged it off. 'Like adults can do anything to help,' she said, sounding unusually like a teenager. 'Everything is so easy for adults. They don't understand a thing about teenagers. Especially girls.' She gave a little shudder.

Lal sat for a moment in silence, the enormity of what her sister was saying weighing on her. 'Bel. I'm so sorry . . . '

'You don't need to be sorry! You just need to help me work out a way to stay here with Gran.'

Lal looked at her in despair. She was sure this wasn't the answer to Bel's problems, but she suddenly felt out of her depth.

Francie waited until Bridget had gone for her afternoon lie-down before she made the call to Hamish. It still felt strange to be phoning him. He'd never been one for chatting on the phone when she was home in Strathan, but she supposed that was because they saw each other so often. Now he had taken to calling her at least twice a week. This was the first time she had phoned him, though, and she felt bad because she was only doing so because she needed a favour.

'Lal and Bel's mum and dad were visiting Tigh na Mara for the weekend and she had just remembered she had promised her son, Peter, she would clear the yard beside the house before his next visit. Bill had so loved tinkering with things, whether it be an ancient tractor or a third-hand plough, and these things had accumulated over the years. Peter said they were an eyesore and he had been trying to persuade her to get rid of them since soon after his father's death. He even said there was money in scrap metal these days.

Francie didn't believe that, but she did think she had better make some move towards keeping her promise.

She and Hamish had a nice chat about the weather and how it was affecting the growing, and the lambs. It was lovely to be able to talk to someone about things like that. Then she moved on to the favour.

'You know you once said you could borrow a trailer and move some of the things that Bill left around the house?'

'Aye, of course. I said you'd only to ask.'

'I don't like to presume, but I wondered if you could move some of it before the weekend? I don't know what you'd do with it, but if you could make a start at clearing it I'm sure it would stop Peter nagging me.'

'Ah, Peter's visiting, is he? I'm surprised he and his wife haven't been up sooner to see young Bel.'

'They're very busy, and they know Lal is doing a good job looking after her.' Francie was quick to excuse her son. She knew that once he made the long journey to Strathan he was always glad to be here, but he worked such long hours it was difficult for him to get away from Glasgow.

'Aye, well, as you say. How's about I bring some of the bigger pieces from Tigh na Mara round here? I've a wee notion to get someone up from Ullapool to see some of my own stuff, maybe put a price on it. He could do it all at the same time.'

'I don't want to be a nuisance, and that just means having the things in the way at your place rather than mine.'

'It'll just be for a wee while, and Peter won't see it here, that's the main thing, isn't it?'

'If you're sure you don't mind . . . '

'Not at all. I'm always glad of the chance to drop in on the girls. As I said, they're doing a fine job of keeping your garden going. And Lal is arranging the

94

first meeting of her Historical Society, has she told you about that?'

'She did mention it. I hope she's not taking too much on.'

'She's managing fine. I think Margery phoning with ideas two or three times a day isn't quite what she was expecting, but it's good to have people enthusiastic, is it no'?'

'Yes, of course,' said Francie doubtfully. She wished more than ever that Bridget was back to reasonable health and she could hurry home to her own life.

'I'll get on to moving those things today or tomorrow. Just let me know if there's anything else I can do for you.'

'You're very kind, Hamish.' For a moment Francie felt almost tearful. He really was such a nice man.

'Och, it's nothing. We're all missing you. It'll be grand when we have you back.' As though embarrassed at expressing so much emotion, Hamish then hurried to ring off.

Lally was looking forward to her parents' visit. Really she was. It was over six weeks since she had seen them last and although they'd chatted regularly on the phone, that wasn't the same as seeing each other in the flesh.

It was good of them to make the long journey up to Strathan, especially when they would be involved in the end of term rush. She just hoped they weren't going to be too cross about Bel's crazy idea of moving to Strathan, or question Lal very closely about her own future plans.

They arrived late on the Friday evening and when, by Saturday morning, things were still going smoothly, Lal breathed a sigh of relief. Maybe her parents weren't going to start interfering. But, just in case, she decided the best form of defence was attack. She suggested a walk down in the direction of Harbour House. She had an idea about the place she wanted to share with them.

'What is Sandy's nephew like?' asked her mother as they opened the gate to Harbour House and wandered into the unkempt garden. 'I take it he hasn't been back since that first visit?'

'No, he hasn't,' said Bel. 'And he didn't even leave us a contact phone number so we can't ask when he is planning to come.'

'Not that it's anything to do with us,' said Lal quickly.

'He was actually quite nice,' said Bel, returning to the original question. 'Once he relaxed a bit I really liked him. He was interested in things, and he knew lots about the Internet which was brilliant.'

'I didn't know you were interested in computers,' said their father, who was keenly interested himself and disappointed at his daughters' lack of appreciation of technological wonders.

Lal jumped in, before Bel could air her thoughts on home-schooling. 'It's not so much being interested, but it would be good to be able to use the

Internet out here as easily as in a city. This guy, Iain, seemed to think that might be possible.'

'Do you think he's going to come and live here?' asked her mother, always more interested in people than technology.

'I'm pretty sure he won't,' said Lal. 'Which has started me thinking about what might happen to Harbour House.'

'It's a shame Sandy didn't leave it to your gran, we always thought he would.'

'It was his choice to leave it to anyone he wanted, Gran's said that more than once. The thing is, if he puts it on the market, I was thinking maybe we should buy it. As a family.' She held her breath. She was fairly sure her mother's reaction would be negative, but she really had no idea what her father might say.

'That is a brilliant idea,' said Bel, jumping in as usual. 'Then we can organise to have the house done up and once Lal has had a few years working at the university in Edinburgh she can come back here and open the museum. Maybe we could even use one of the outbuildings as the museum? And there would always be somewhere for you and Mum to stay when you come to visit Gran. You'd like that, wouldn't you, Dad? Tigh na Mara can be a bit of a squash.'

'And where are we going to get all this money?' said their father.

'Oh . . . ' said Bel, looking crestfallen.

'I wondered about a mortgage,' said Lal hesitantly. 'I wouldn't be able to afford it on my own, even if I get this job, but I could contribute. And I thought maybe you could too? You did once offer to buy a flat in Edinburgh when I was studying there, you said property was a good investment.'

'Edinburgh is an entirely different kettle of fish to Strathan.'

'But think how brilliant it would be in the long run,' said Bel, back in full flow. 'You could retire up here, you've always said you wanted to take early retirement, haven't you? And you could do bed and breakfast like Sandy planned to do. I think that would be fantastic.'

'Strathan is all right for a holiday,' said their mother, looking pale. 'But it's really not my idea of a nice place to live. Especially in winter.' She shivered. 'Even at this time of year it isn't exactly warm. We've got a lovely house in Glasgow, why would we want to move?'

'You wouldn't have to move,' said Lal. 'You could think of it as an investment.'

'And Lal and I do want to live here. Maybe we could buy it off you, once we're earning money.'

Lal glared at her sister. It was all very well having her support for this crazy idea, but now wasn't the time to talk to their parents about staying in Strathan.

Their father looked around at the ruined buildings, and then at the low hills behind and the blue water of the bay in front, stretching to the high mountains of the north. 'It's strange to think of you girls liking it here so much. Would you really want to live here?'

'Yes!' said Bel.

'If it was feasible,' said Lally, more cautiously.

Peter shook his head in confusion. 'When I was young, all anyone wanted to do was leave. And I can't help thinking you'd be wasting your talents, stuck away out here, Alicia. It's all very well helping your gran out over the summer, but long term? I'm not sure I think it's a good idea.'

Lal opened her mouth to argue, then saw her mother's expression. She looked absolutely appalled. Lal sighed and turned the conversation to other matters.

Lally's Idea Takes Shape

Iain had been back in Edinburgh almost a month now and yet still his thoughts kept straying to Strathan, and Harbour House. And the two girls who lived at Tigh na Mara. He couldn't believe that young people like that existed in this day and age. Hard-working and satisfied — no, not just satisfied, happy — to be way out in the middle of nowhere.

There was something so genuine about them, he couldn't help contrasting that with the surface politeness of his colleagues and neighbours. If he hadn't met the Dunmore girls, he was sure he would have been quite content with this, but now it felt as though something was missing.

He wondered if he could fit in another visit to Strathan, but before he did that, he needed to speak to his parents and find out more about Great

Uncle Alex, or Sandy as he was referred to up here.

His mother phoned him as usual at the weekend. When she raised the topic of Harbour House, again, it gave him just the opening he needed.

'No, I haven't decided what to do about the place yet. Which reminds me, can you and Dad tell me anything more about Great Uncle Alex? Do you know what made him move up there?'

'I've no idea. I never even met the man. The family argument or whatever it was happened long before I knew your father. You could speak to your dad about it if you want?'

Iain hesitated. 'Isn't it still a bit of a sore point? The property being left to me?'

'You have to admit it was rather odd, but your father is used to the idea now. He's away getting the Sunday paper. I'll get him to give you a ring when he gets back, shall I?'

Iain agreed to this and then wondered what he had let himself in for. He and his father rarely spoke over the phone, neither of them were the chatty type.

When his father called, he came straight to the point. 'You wanted to talk to me about your Great Uncle Alex?'

'Yes. I . . . ' It was hard to know where to start. Iain tried again. 'When I was up in Sutherland the neighbours showed me some photographs of him. He looked so like Grandad. Thinner and fitter, but very alike. It was a shock to see them and I wondered why I had never known him.'

'I never knew him either,' said his father defensively.

'What happened? Why did he and Grandad fall out?'

'It was never discussed, but I think it was to do with the business. You know Grandad took over the factory from his father? It's always been a family business.'

'Yes, I know.' Iain was just grateful that his older brother, Stephen, was sufficiently interested to want to continue the tradition. He personally couldn't awaken any enthusiasm for carpet manufacturing. 'So you think it was about money?'

'As I said, I'm not sure. I know there was an argument about my Uncle Alex going into the Navy. He joined as a raw recruit, didn't even go in as an officer. The argument must have been pretty bad because as I understand it the family never really spent time together again.'

'He didn't even come to his brother — our grandad's — funeral, did he?' Iain had been too young to wonder about that at the time, but now it seemed very strange.

'Oh yes, he came back for that. And I believe he had been back for his own parents' funerals, although I'm too young to remember.'

'I thought you said you didn't know him!'

'I didn't know him. I didn't say I hadn't met him. But he never stayed around after the event, never came to the house or anything. We just assumed he didn't want anything to do with the family, which was why it was such a shock when he left the property to you.'

'Ye-es,' said Iain. It had certainly been that. He almost felt sorry for his father, these mysteries clearly made him uncomfortable. It wasn't his fault his father and uncle had fallen out so irreconcilably.

On the spur of the moment he said, 'Why don't you and Mum come up and visit sometime? See the place for yourself? It would be good for you to have a holiday.'

'Well, that's very kind of you,' said his father, doubtfully, and Iain wished he hadn't made the suggestion. 'We don't want to make decisions too hastily, do we? I'll chat it over with your mother and see when we can get away. Things are very busy at the factory just now. I can't just leave Stephen to see to everything.'

Iain stopped feeling sorry for his

father and returned to his usual feeling of irritation. Why was work always so much more important than family? He ended the call, brooding over this fact. He bet Lal and Bel's parents always made time for them.

If his parents didn't want to accompany him, there was no reason why he shouldn't make a brief trip up to Strathan himself. He would check how things were at work next week and see when he could fit it in.

* * *

Lal was making broth on the Sunday morning when her mother appeared in the doorway.

'Lal! What's this about Bel wanting to stay in Strathan long term? She says she's spoken to you about it and she says she's serious! I can't believe you've been discussing this without saying a word to us.'

Lal sighed and pushed the pan to the rear of the Rayburn and moved the kettle forward. This called for tea.

'I'm sorry. She's told you, has she? I keep thinking she'll come to her senses. I was hoping that seeing you this weekend would make her realise how much she misses Glasgow. And you, of course.'

'She says she doesn't miss Glasgow at all! She says she hates school and never wants to go back there. Lal, what on earth is going on?'

Lal brought two steaming mugs to the table and her mother took one and sat down, cradling it in her hands. She looked bewildered.

'She's told me a little bit about school,' Lally said carefully. 'It seems there have been, er, problems there for a while.'

'I know she was never as keen as you and Anthony, but she's always done well academically. If she disliked it so much, why didn't she say?'

Lal took a deep breath. 'Mum, I think she was being bullied. And it's hard to talk about something like that.

Apparently. I don't know much, I just know she's desperate not to go back.'

'Bullied! Annabel!' Her mother shook her head in disbelief. 'What was happening? Why didn't she say anything?'

'I don't know, Mum. I just know that you'll need to sort that out before Bel will even consider moving back.'

'I'm not going back,' said Bel, appearing in the doorway. 'I've told you, Mum. I don't need to go to school. I can do all the studying I need here, and I'll be a great help to Gran.'

Sally put a hand out to her younger daughter. 'Bel, why didn't you tell us anything was wrong?'

Bel shrugged uncomfortably. After a moment she said quietly, 'I didn't really realise anything was wrong for ages. I thought it was just me.' She shook her head. 'When people tell you constantly you're odd, you just kind of accept it. It's only when I came to stay out here that I thought, actually, I don't have to accept it.'

'Odd? Odd? Who says you are odd? Where's your father? We need to get on to the school immediately and get this sorted out.'

'You can contact the school if you like,' said Bel, her pale face solemn. 'I don't care what you do. But I'm not going back there.'

And she retained that implacable position throughout the rest of the day. Her father might say that it was best to go and face your demons, but Bel maintained she wasn't interested. 'It's all in the past,' she said stubbornly. 'I'm moving on.'

'We could find you another school if you really didn't want to go back there,' said her mother. 'You don't have to move all the way to Strathan to avoid these people.'

'But Mum, I want to live in Strathan. Don't you remember when we were talking about buying Harbour House? I thought you understood. This is where I want to be.'

Her parents shot Lal a look of

reproach. They clearly thought her ideas about Harbour House were a bad example to her sister.

'And what does your gran think?' said their father coldly. 'Is she in on this too?'

'I haven't spoken to her yet,' admitted Bel. 'But I'm sure she won't mind. She likes having me here, she said so.'

'Having you to stay for a few weeks is quite different to having you here permanently. Your gran has her own life to live.'

'I don't think she'd mind,' said Bel, but for the first time she sounded uncertain.

'I've a good mind to take you back to Glasgow with us in the morning, sort this foolishness out at once.'

'You can't do that! I won't go! And anyway, I need to be here to help Lal. I do, don't I Lal?'

Eventually it was decided that Bel would stay at Tigh na Mara for the time being, but her parents were adamant she should return to Glasgow for the beginning of the new term. In the meantime they were going to contact her old school and look around for a new one for her. Bel listened to these arrangements in silence. Lal suspected it was that she had got what she wanted for the time being — a summer at Strathan. She didn't believe, despite her parents' insistence, that the child had given up her dream of staying here for good.

★　★　★

Lally was preparing for the first meeting of the Strathan Historical Society. It was to be held in the village hall. Bel had designed posters advertising the event and Margery had arranged for these to be displayed as far afield as Inverloch. They had provoked a fair amount of comment, but Lally had no idea how many people might actually turn up.

She flicked nervously through her notes, and wondered for the twentieth time whether this really was a good idea. Why did she think she could talk to people about their own area? People like Hamish knew twice as much as she did, she was being ridiculous setting this up.

The outer door banged and Bel, who had been scouting for arrivals, appeared. 'Ishbel is talking to some man I don't recognise and Hamish's jeep is just coming down the Drummore Road. So that's at least three people as well as us.'

'Hmm,' said Lally. She wasn't sure she actually wanted anyone to come. If the first meeting was a disaster, she wouldn't have to continue. At this moment that sounded like the best thing that could happen.

'There's another car,' continued Bel, peering out of the window. 'I think it's Margery and her husband. I didn't think he'd come along, did you? And here's someone else . . . No, they're not parking. Oh, they're dropping two girls off. Gosh, you really have provoked a lot of interest.'

Bel came back and sat at the table beside Lally, as though she too was feeling nervous.

'It's all thanks to your brilliant posters. Goodness, I hope they don't expect me to do all the talking, I hope people will come with ideas of their own.'

'Hamish said you did really well when you spoke to the Hall Committee.'

'Yes, but that was people I knew. Oh dear, here they come . . .'

Lal took a deep breath and fixed a smile on her face as the first arrivals made there way inside.

She and Bel had set out a table in the centre of the hall and put a number of chairs around it. The problem was, as they had no idea how many people would turn up, they hadn't known how many chairs they would need. As the door clicked open once again it was clear they had underestimated. Lally rose and brought over more seats from the side where they were stacked. There were ten people here now. No, make that twelve. Which was a very good thing, wasn't it?

She waited until the trickle of arrivals finally stopped, and then smiled around and took another deep breath.

'Hello everyone. I'm delighted to welcome you all here tonight for this first meeting of the Strathan Historical Society — although as this is a first meeting one of the things we should do is decide on a name, and if you don't like that one we can discuss others . . . '

'It's a good old-fashioned name,' said the man who had come in with Ishbel. He sounded pompous, but Lally smiled encouragingly, trying to place him. From one of the new bungalows by the beach at Clashnessie maybe.

'We'll stick with that for now then, but I'm still open to suggestions. Now, I thought I'd set out a few of my ideas for how the group might run, but if anyone wants to contribute feel free to speak up.'

'Far better if you set everything out for them,' said the pompous man. 'I can't be doing with this modern consensus way of doing things.'

Bel sniggered and Lally smiled through gritted teeth. 'I'll just get on then, shall I?'

After that, thank goodness, he stopped interrupting, and Lally found herself getting into her stride.

On the whole, the meeting went quite well. It was a shame there weren't more young, or youngish, people. Apart from the two teenage girls, who were apparently doing Higher History at the school in Ullapool, the average age of the newcomers was over sixty. The pompous man, whose name was Arthur, was a little too fond of the sound of his own voice, but Lally encouraged the others to chip in.

Hamish was very helpful, making suggestions in his measured way which were almost always adopted by the group. Margery was more interested in things like how often they should meet, and whether they should arrange refreshments.

It was agreed they should meet fortnightly. They would begin each meeting with a talk on an area of local history, the first one to be given by Lally herself. There was also definite interest in some trips to local historical sites.

In fact, things had gone so well that, against her better judgement, Lally found herself mentioning her dream of a local museum. 'Of course, that would have to be in the future.'

'A long way in the future,' said Ishbel firmly.

'But I wondered what everyone thought of the idea?' For some reason Ishbel's negativity made Lally want to push harder.

'Would we have anything to display?' asked Margery.

'Yes, definitely. For example, I've already got that Victorian pottery and the coins I showed you. It doesn't need to be finds of nationwide significance, just items of local interest.'

'I've family photos going back to the 1890s,' offered Hamish. 'Of course, maybe they wouldn't be of interest to anyone but me, but if you'd like to see them . . . '

'That sounds brilliant,' said Lally gratefully. 'It's fascinating to see the way people dressed in those days. And it might give us some insight into how the land was worked then, if they were taken outdoors.'

'Actually, I've got something rather more interesting than that,' said Arthur. 'Been keeping it to myself, but perhaps now is the time to show it to a wider audience.' He paused to make sure he had their full attention. Lally suspected he was going to announce the discovery of yet another ruined black house, but smiled encouragingly.

'I have in my possession,' he said, 'what I am reliably informed is a ceremonial Neolithic axe head, found locally.'

Lally took a sharp breath. From the blank expressions around the table, only possibly Hamish understood the significance of this. 'You mean a replica, I presume?' she suggested.

'I most certainly do not! As many of you know, my wife and I have holidayed in this area for years before we eventually moved here. On one of those visits I happened to spot what I thought was an unusual looking stone on the slopes above Clashnessie. I took it home and in due course managed to have it identified by a friend of mine. It is a polished ceremonial axe head, probably from around 3500 BC. Now what do you think of that?'

Lally felt faint with shock. If what he claimed was true this was, as far as she knew, the first such find on the area. It had great significance. It was also Treasure Trove, and as such belonged to the Crown. It should have been handed in immediately!

'That sounds fascinating,' she said heartily. 'I presume you've reported it to the appropriate authorities? I'm surprised they didn't make something of it, a press release at least.'

'Hmm, hmm.' Arthur cleared his throat. 'Actually, no, I haven't reported it to anyone. I didn't see any need. They have thousands of these things from all over the British Isles.'

'But not from Strathan! This could tell us something new about who inhabited the area in Neolithic times. In fact, I'm not sure we have definite proof the area was inhabited then. The museums need to know.'

'I found the thing, so it's mine,' said the little man, starting to look bullish. 'I wouldn't mind it being exhibited locally, but I know what happens when you give these things to national museums, they're just put in a cupboard somewhere and forgotten.'

'Not exactly,' said Lally, thinking of the days and weeks she had spent cataloguing such finds last year, to make sure they weren't forgotten.

'Sounds like a fine thing you have there,' said Hamish. 'It's grand of you to tell us about it.'

'Hmm,' said Arthur, looking as though he wished he hadn't.

'You will report it to the authorities

now, won't you?' said Lally. 'Can you remember exactly when and where you found it? All these things are important.'

'I don't see why I should . . . '

'You should if it's the law,' said Ishbel. So far, she had been nodding approvingly at all the nit-picking little comments. Arthur had made, but now she looked concerned.

'We've only this young lady's word for it that it is the law.'

'Lally knows these things!' said Bel, her loyalty making her speak out for the first time since the start of the meeting. 'She's worked in a big museum. Of course she's right.'

'I'll make my own enquiries,' said the man, and refused to be drawn further.

Lally decided now was a good time to end the meeting, before there were any more worrying revelations.

She and Bel stayed behind to help Ishbel tidy up.

'I think that went brilliantly,' said Bel, happily stacking chairs. 'Loads of people turned up. Even some young-sters, although they probably won't come again.'

'It was certainly better attended than I expected,' allowed Ishbel. 'Perhaps it isn't such a bad idea. I do like to see the village hall being used.'

'Lets hope they don't shut us down before we've even started for harbour-ing an illegal cache of Treasure Trove.' Lal shuddered at how horrified her former colleagues at the National Museum would be if they had heard Arthur's announcement. And what if, even now, he refused to hand the item over? Was she then obliged to tell them herself? That would be a really good start to promoting support for her little project.

Francie Returns

Francie was delighted to be finally going home. The weeks looking after Bridget had seemed endless. She was, of course, pleased to have been able to help. It was only right that she supported her sister, and a shame Bridget didn't have any children or grandchildren of her own to take an interest. But now her younger sibling seemed to be on the mend — at least enough to start resenting Francie running the flat for her — and after ensuring that daily help was available, Francie had been relieved to head back to her own life.

She drove the little Skoda carefully along the winding roads of Sutherland. It was July now and there were plenty of tourists about, which meant you really had to pay attention. It wasn't easy for these foreign campervans to negotiate main roads which were only single track. Francie smiled to herself as she swung on to the road north of Inverloch. This was even narrower than ever, but she knew every twist and turn.

She waved as she paused to let two cars pass in the opposite direction and recognised her neighbours. Oh, how good it was to be amongst people she knew!

At the village hall she hesitated and then, instead of turning left for Tigh na Mara, she continued straight. After half a mile she drew up before a neat little cottage that sheltered in the lee of a rocky hill.

She climbed slowly out of the car, feeling stiff after all those hours of driving. Nobody appeared from the house and she began to feel a little foolish. Hamish had mentioned during the last of their frequent phone calls he was looking forward to seeing her again, but he probably didn't expect her to call in even before she had returned to Tigh na Mara.

She couldn't see him in the nearby fields and had just decided to try the house, although it was so unlike him to be inside at this time of day, when the side door swung open.

'Francie! It's you!'

Hamish made as though to move forward and then hesitated, hovering on the top step. That was so like him Francie felt her heart beat in a strange way, as though she really was back where she belonged. She smiled up at her friend, noting he hadn't changed at all, from the greying curly hair to the darned woollen jersey. And although he had been almost chatty over the phone, he was now back to being tongue-tied.

She had been going to hug him, but realised just in time how embarrassed he would be. Instead she patted him in the arm. It's good to see you again.'

'And you.' If she hadn't known him better she would have thought his weather beaten face had blushed. 'And, er, have you time for a wee cup of tea? I happen to have some of those oat

125

biscuits you like so much.'

'How could I refuse? And you can fill me in on all the gossip I've missed whilst I've been away. Phone calls are never the same.'

Francie followed him happily through to the kitchen at the back of the house. There was no view from here which was perhaps why Hamish's mother had spent so little time in here. Maybe she should suggest to Hamish he should knock the kitchen through to the front room, it would be wonderful with that lovely out-look towards Wester Ross. For now, however, she settled down on an upright chair and prepared to catch up on real life.

* * *

Lally was thankful her grandmother was finally returning to Strathan. She had been glad to help out by looking after the croft and Bel, and doing all the chores Gran seemed to take on and accomplish so effortlessly. But it had been hard work and she was glad it was nearly over. How did Gran, who was now nearing seventy, manage? Lally was filled once again with love and admiration for the older woman.

She and Bel had just finished cleaning the little house. It had grown surprisingly grubby during the weeks they had been in charge and they wanted to get it back to Gran's high standards.

Lal plumped herself down in one of the cane chairs in conservatory with a sigh of relief. 'Phew! Thank goodness that's done.'

'Just don't go remembering yet another corner we haven't dusted or bed we haven't vacuumed under.'

'As long as you don't remember yet another outbuilding we need to sweep out!'

'I don't think there are any more out-buildings. Thank goodness. Who knew a small place could take so much tidying?' Bel sat down and stretched luxuriously. Lal was pleased to see how well she looked. She had stopped wear-ing a scarf over her hair in that strange gypsy fashion and she had some colour in her cheeks.

'I suppose once Gran's home I'll need to think about what I'm going to do with myself,' mused Lal. 'I've been here two months.'

'But you want to stay longer, don't you?'

'If it was practical . . . ' Lal allowed her eyes to wander across the fields that spread out below them and to the bay beyond. They'd been remarkably lucky with the weather this summer and it was yet another brilliantly sunny day.

'Well, stay for now at least. You've already put in your application for the job at the university. You don't need to go back until they offer you an interview. And I'm planning to move into the little back room like I said.'

Lal sighed. 'Mum is hoping you'll go back south soon. She's longing to see you again.'

Bel pulled a face. 'They were here a couple of weekends ago, they know I'm fine.'

'Yes, but they want you home.'

'Lal, this is my home now.' Bel was starting to look mutinous. They hadn't had this debate since their parents' visit and Lal had begun to hope her sister had realised how unrealistic her plans were.

'This is Gran's home, actually. How do you know she'd be happy for you to stay? And, in any case, Mum and Dad are serious about you being back in Glasgow when school starts again in August.'

'I'm not going back to school, I told you.'

'Bel, I'm more sorry than I can say about what happened to you, and I wish you'd told us sooner . . . '

Bel shook her head, switched on and focussed again. 'Don't worry about that, it's all in the past. What matters is now and finding a way for me to stay here.'

Lally was sure there was some answer to this, some argument she should put forward as to why Bel should return to

Glasgow and face down these girls, but before she could frame the words there was the sound of a car putt-putting up the road and then, with a final struggle, turning into their yard.

'Gran!' shouted Bel, springing up from her chair and racing out of the open door as though she was four rather than fourteen.

Lal went out to meet her grandmother more slowly, but equally relieved to have her home. Gran was good at sorting things out.

★ ★ ★

Francie was so happy to be home. Tears rose to her eyes as she hugged her darling girls to her, fended off an excited Pup and took in the house and the garden and the bay all at the same time. She didn't know why she had taken that little detour to see Hamish. Nice as it had been to see him again it was wonderful to be here.

'How is everything? Are the hens

laying? I see the lambs are doing marvellously, they're so big.'

'Oh Gran, it's lovely to have you back,' said Lal, hugging her tight and sounding more relieved than Francie would have expected.

She returned the hugs, ruffled Bel's hair for the last time and turned to bring in her luggage.

After the first words Lal seemed to settle back into her old self. She ran through all the jobs she had done, as organised and capable as she had always been. Francie had never doubted that her granddaughters would manage, but even she was impressed at quite how much had been achieved. The plants in the greenhouse weren't just still alive, they were flourishing and half had been planted out in the lazy beds. The good weather would have helped, but Lal must have green fingers to have achieved so much. It was a shame she didn't have an outlet for this skill back in her city life.

'How was the journey?' asked Lally.

'It's a long way. I hope you stopped for a break?'

'Of course. I had a flask of coffee with me and sandwiches for lunch, I stopped a couple of times.' For some reason Francie didn't mention she had also stopped less than half an hour ago, at Hamish McDougall's. It was probably because the girls wouldn't be interested in that.

Eventually, after unpacking the car and taking a brief tour of the fields, they were all seated comfortably in the conservatory, drinking numerous cups of tea and enjoying a fruitcake Bel had baked.

'I'm not sure you need me back,' Francie joked. 'The garden and animals are doing wonderfully and clearly my role as family baker is under threat from this young lady.'

Bel smiled broadly, showing her braces. Francie did hope the dentist would remove these soon, it couldn't be good for the child's confidence to have a mouthful of iron. She was amazingly self-assured with adults, but Francie was aware she tended to avoid youngsters.

'There were two of us here and we only just managed. We don't know how you do it all on your own,' Bel said.

'She's right,' said Lal. 'Are you sure you haven't taken too much on here? It must have been a nice rest to only have Aunty Bridget's flat to look after.'

'You forget I also had to look after Aunty Bridget,' said Francie, and then felt guilty when the two girls giggled. 'Not that I'm complaining, it can't be easy suffering all the health problems she's had over the years.'

'She rather makes the most of them,' said Lal.

Secretly, Francie agreed, but she said loyally, 'She's had a lot to put up with. But the doctors are pleased with the progress she's making now, which is a good thing.'

'And you're home!' said Bel, bouncing in her chair. 'Now everything will be back to normal and we can plan.'

Francie saw a shadow pass over her older granddaughter's face and wondered what this was all about. She was pleased to be home and to have such a welcome, but she wasn't so sure about 'plans'. What was Bel up to now?

★   ★   ★

Iain had finally found time for a second visit to Harbour House. He shouldn't really be going, he had more than enough to keep him busy in Edinburgh. The new job was challenging to say the least. In fact, his predecessor had left things in rather a mess. And he was enjoying stretching himself, sorting things out. Yet all the time, at the back of his mind, was the picture of the little bothy and the ruined house and the wide blue bay.

Somehow, he needed to go back and see if it was still as tantalising.

He also wondered if the young woman, Lally, was still house-sitting for her grandmother next door.

Eventually he managed to free up some time and set off early one morning, heading north up the A9. The journey went well and he was driving along the single track road north of Inverloch soon after one o'clock. His spirits lifted, yes actually lifted, as he turned the last corner and saw the natural stone archway reaching out into the sea and then the silhouette of Harbour House. Maybe he could understand what had drawn his great uncle here.

He didn't like to stare at Tigh an Mara, but he couldn't help noticing that the little Fiat he had taken to be Lally's car was now accompanied by a very old Skoda. Did this mean the grandmother was home? In which case, maybe Lally wouldn't be staying much longer. He was glad he had decided on this visit. He wondered whether he could reasonably pop up to the house that very afternoon and say hello. It would be the neighbourly thing to do, wouldn't it?

He made himself a quick lunch, which he ate sitting on the little patio outside the bothy, drinking in the view. Normally he would have been reading a paper or checking his computer whilst he ate, but here it seemed to be enough just to sit. Probably he was tired after the long drive.

As soon as he'd tidied away the meal and unpacked the few possessions he had brought with him, he headed up the lane to the little white house of his neighbours.

He was greeted not by Lally, or the exuberant Bel, but by a grey-haired woman with the same lanky build and generous smile who could only be their grandmother.

'You must be Sandy's great nephew!' she said, taking his hand in both hers and examining him with keen interest. 'I'm so pleased to meet you. Bel has told me all about you. I was hoping it wouldn't be too long before you visited again.'

Iain found himself smiling in return.

'I couldn't resist the chance of a few days up here, especially when the weather promised to be so good.'

'Ye-es,' she said, nodding thoughtfully. 'You haven't seen the place at its worst yet, have you? It's lovely now, but you need to see it in all weathers to really understand it.'

'I see,' said Iain, although actually he didn't.

'When the gales are howling round and the rain lashing the windows and the waves are up so high you think they'll wash the jetty away . . . When you've seen Strathan like that you've really seen it.'

The woman actually seemed to relish the thought of this wild weather, but Iain decided he preferred the place as it was.

'Come in and join me for a cup of tea,' she said, drawing him inside. 'Lally and Bel are away tidying one of the holiday cottages for me, they said it was too soon for me to take that on again just yet. Such good girls. So we have all the time in the world to chat.'

Iain followed her inside with some trepidation. He suspected he was going to be subject to rather more questions than he would have liked.

★ ★ ★

'We've got to approach her tonight,' said Bel. 'Whilst she's still over the moon about being home and grateful for all we've done for her.'

The two girls were walking back from a cottage half a mile from Tigh na Mara. It belonged to a family who lived in Perth and was let out to holidaymakers for most of the year. Francie had undertaken to do the cleaning and linen changes between visitors, an arrangement that allowed her to earn a little money and satisfy her curiosity about any newcomers to the area.

Lal wasn't nearly as enthusiastic as her grandmother about taking on this chore, but for once it had been an easy changeover. Lally was coming to love clean and tidy holidaymakers!

Both girls were in a good mood as they followed the road along the contour of the hill back towards Tigh na Mara.

'Bel, I really don't think this is a good idea.' Lally sighed, her pleasure at a job easily accomplished diminished as she thought of the family difficulties ahead. 'Mum and Dad aren't going to agree to you staying. If you involve Gran you're just putting her in an awkward position.'

'I'm just sounding her out at the moment. If she agrees, Mum and Dad are far more likely to see sense themselves. And we have to ask her about you staying for the rest of the summer.'

'I need to find work to support myself.' She sighed at the thought, but it was good to be realistic.

'Don't be so negative,' said Bel severely. 'Gran's going to give us all the money from doing the holiday cottages whilst she's been away. I'll give you my share, I don't need it for anything. That'll keep you going for a while. You know, I think it's probably a good thing you haven't heard any more about that university job, it would take you away from here at a really important time.'

Lally sighed. She had tried not to put too much hope into her application, but she couldn't deny she was disappointed to have heard nothing. She knew the university was renowned for its slow administration, but it was over a month now since the closing date for applications. 'If I don't hear by the end of the week, I'll definitely give up on it,' she said, trying to sound as though this was perfectly fine.

'And you will stay here at least until the end of the summer, won't you? Go on, Lal, say you will . . . '

Lally gave her little sister a mock punch. 'I'll think about it. If you stop nagging.'

Bel punched her back and they were both giggling as they rounded the corner to the conservatory and found Gran and Iain Cunningham ensconced in the cane chairs, chatting as though they had known each other for years. Lally felt obscurely hurt. The man had never looked as relaxed and happy when he visited her.

'Girls, look who's here,' said Gran, gesturing to the visitor. 'Isn't it lucky that I'm home for Iain's second visit? I've been so looking forward to meeting him after all you've told me.'

Lally was pleased to see that Iain looked a little uncomfortable at this effusiveness. She smiled a polite hello, but Bel was already jumping in.

'You're back! That's brilliant! Now you can explain to me properly how to get an Internet connection via a mobile phone. Or better still, how we get broadband working here. You're just the person I need to speak to.'

'Broadband?' said Gran, puzzled.

'Yes. It's a way of connecting to the Internet that allows faster download speeds and doesn't interfere with your telephone line.'

'Bel, my dear, I may be past my prime, but I do know what broadband is. What I don't understand is how it can be possible to get it out here? We made enquiries a year or two ago and the phone companies were very unhelpful.'

'Technology is changing rapidly, it might be worth pursuing this again,' said Iain.

Lal sighed as she saw the enthusiasm with which all three of them were going to discuss this subject. 'I'll go and make a fresh pot of tea, shall I?' she said.

She was pleased to withdraw to the privacy of the kitchen where Pup followed in hope of a biscuit. Iain's unexpected reappearance had thrown her. She didn't know why. Probably because she was still worrying about her little sister. It was hard to accept that Bel had been so unhappy at school and that none of the family had noticed.

She sighed again, loudly now there was no one to hear her. Improved

142

Internet access was just what she didn't want to hear about, it would only make Bel more intent on her home-schooling idea.

However, by the time the kettle had boiled and she had re-laid the tray, she had decided there was no point in worrying about that now. She would encourage Iain to stay and eat with them, that would keep Gran occupied and, hopefully, prevent Bel introducing any controversial subjects.

* * *

The third meeting of the Strathan Historical Society was the following evening. Lal was delighted that Gran was able to come along, and delighted also that she wasn't going to be doing most of the talking this time. Hamish had arranged to bring along an elderly neighbour who could remember what it was like to farm before mechanisation had reached their part of the country. He was, according to Bel, 'absolutely ancient', but he had a wealth of knowledge about the local area and Lal was delighted he had been persuaded to attend.

She wondered if the man, Arthur, would appear. He hadn't come to the second meeting and she still couldn't decide what she should do about the find he claimed was a Neolithic axe head. She really needed to see it before she spoke to anyone else. It wasn't impossible that he had identified the thing incorrectly. And she really didn't want to report him to the authorities, it felt so much like telling tales. And yet if it really was what he claimed, the museums needed to know.

She had chatted to Gran about it a little in the afternoon and Gran suggested trying persuasion one more time. 'I'm sure you can get him to see sense,' she had said. Lal wasn't so sure herself, but was pleased to have shared her concerns.

At first it didn't seem that Arthur would turn up. In that case, she and

Gran had agreed they would visit him at home, the idea of which made Lal very nervous. Then, at the last moment, he joined the group in the village hall. Lal and Gran exchanged relieved looks. His willingness to attend must be a good sign, mustn't it?

The talk by Hamish's elderly neighbour was excellent. Lal hoped she was this alert and interesting when she was nearly ninety! The youngsters were particularly fascinated by his stories and the old photographs he and Hamish handed around. The two History Higher students had continued to attend the meeting, despite Bel's predictions, and one of them said this was the best history lesson she had ever had. Even Bel, who still tended to avoid the girls, looked impressed at that.

While some of the group were once again debating whether future meetings should involve refreshments (Ishbel was opposed as she knew all the work would fall to her, Margery thought it was a super idea as it would encourage people to socialise more), Lal and Gran homed in on Arthur.

'Lovely to see you again,' said Gran brightly. 'How is your wife keeping?'

Arthur replied positively, but was already looking around for a means of escape. Gran was having none of this.

'Lal was telling me about this wonderful find you have made,' she continued. 'What was it? A stone something? An axe?'

Arthur couldn't prevent himself from correcting her. 'A ceremonial Neolithic axe head. Polished stone. Very impressive.'

'I'd love to see it,' said Lal. 'It sounds fascinating.'

'My granddaughter used to work at the National Museum in Edinburgh, she knows about these things.'

'I suppose if you are interested, you could come round to the house.' Lal could see the man was torn between the desire to show off his find, and his concern it might be taken from him. Poor man, he might as well give in now, he had no chance of turning Gran from her path when she was determined like this.

'We'd really like that. Why don't we pop along tomorrow morning? And if Lal thinks it worthwhile, if it's as special as you both think, then she's just the person to tell you how to have it verified. She knows all the right people to speak to in Edinburgh.'

'But I haven't made my mind up . . . '

'We'll see you tomorrow, then? Would ten-thirty suit you? That's very kind.'

Gran finally stood aside and let the man escape.

'I don't think you'll have any trouble now,' she said happily.

'I hope not. But I'm not a specialist, you know, I don't really know that much.'

'We don't need to tell Arthur that. You know the laws of Treasure Trove, which is the main thing. Now, I'd better go and settle this argument about teas. Really, you'd think Ishbel didn't want that new tea urn to be used.'

* ★ ★

Bel left it until the three of them had returned from the visit to Arthur's bungalow the following morning before finally broaching the subject of her plans.

The visit went surprisingly well. The axe head was more stunning than Francie had expected, a dark polished shaft of stone that was definitely not local. Arthur seemed to have decided to give in with good grace. He said he didn't want to be identified as the finder and let Lal take away the little padded box containing his treasure.

She would now begin the process of declaring the discovery to the correct authorities. Francie was delighted with this outcome, although Lal pronounced herself quite nervous to be in possession of such a rare object.

Bel had been suitably impressed by the ancient artefact, but once they returned home her mind shifted to other things. Francie heard her and

Lally arguing in undertones in the kitchen. 'It's time we told her,' hissed Bel.

Lally was obviously trying to persuade her to wait a little longer, but Francie was getting quite nervous to know what was going on. Better to know the worst, she always felt.

'Is there something I should know?' she said, making both girls start guiltily.

'Well . . . ' said Lal.

'I want to ask you something,' said Bel.

Lal shrugged as though giving in. 'I'll make a pot of tea,' she said.

Bel waited until they were all sitting in the conservatory sipping the hot liquid. Then she dropped her bombshell.

'Gran, you wouldn't mind if I moved here to live with you, would you? Permanently, I mean. That would be OK, wouldn't it?'

Francie stared at the youngster. 'Bel darling, I've loved having you to stay, but it's not practical in the long run.'

Bel lent forward, her face pale and earnest. 'It is practical. I'm going to home-school, that means learning by myself at home. Iain arranging the Internet connection for us fits in perfectly.'

'I can't supervise home-schooling,' said Francie, horrified. She had felt out of her depth academically once Bel's father left primary school. This would certainly be beyond her.

'That's all right, you won't have to,' said Bel kindly. 'I'll do it all myself, with the Internet for support. I know I can do this, Gran. It's not as though school work is difficult at this stage.'

'It isn't?' said Francie, looking to Lally for help.

'It probably isn't if you're Bel,' said the older girl. 'I know Bel is really keen on this and she probably could cope fine, academically, but I'm not sure it's the best thing. It's a big imposition on you, and Mum and Dad were horrified when she mentioned it.'

Francie wasn't at all surprised to hear

150

that. Would Peter and Sally think she had put Bel up to this? They might think she was trying to steal the child from them. How awful. Francie had loved having the company, and had worried she would miss the girls when they left, but she had never thought for a second that they could stay. Francie had become so used to the idea that young people left the Highlands she had long since ceased to question it.

She listened to her youngest grand-child chattering on enthusiastically and the thought began to grow at the back of her mind: why shouldn't they stay? Obviously there was no work for Lal at the moment, but if Bel's ideas about home-schooling proved to be realistic . . .

'Listen, Annabel,' she said, interrupting the flow. 'I'm not saying an outright no, I can see that the idea has some attractions. But I won't agree unless your parents are in favour. You wouldn't expect me to go against their wishes, would you?'

Bel's face fell. 'I don't want you to go

against them, of course not, but I thought if you tried to help me persuade them?'

'I'll discuss it with them. But not immediately. I want time to settle back in here and talk it over with the both of you. We'll bear it in mind as a possibility, but nothing more. Is that clear? My agreement is not a foregone conclusion.'

Bel did her best to smile. Thank goodness the family knew when not to gainsay Francie. 'You're bound to see what a brilliant idea it is, when you've had the chance to think it over,' she said, but not sounding nearly so sure as she had.

A Shock For Hamish

Iain was disappointed at how little he had seen of Lally. He had been back at Harbour House four days now and hadn't had a single conversation with her that didn't involve at least one other person. He enjoyed Francie's company, and Bel was such a funny child you couldn't help liking her, but what he really wanted to was get to know Lally better. He didn't know why. It was as though she was the key to understanding Harbour House, and helping him decide whether to keep or sell it.

He was delighted, therefore, when he called at Tigh na Mara on Thursday morning to ask if he could pick up any shopping in Inverloch and Lally opted instead to accept a lift to town with him. Yes! The journey there and back was the ideal opportunity to get to know this odd and intriguing woman.

To begin with they chatted about the local area and Iain was once again impressed by the knowledge and enthusiasm of the Dunmore women.

In fact, Lally was so keen on telling him why he should spend more time in the area he couldn't help saying, 'I thought you were the one who wanted your family to buy Harbour House? That can hardly happen if I keep it.'

Lally pushed the heavy hair back from her face and frowned. 'That was just Bel talking, you shouldn't take any notice of her. It was just a vague idea.'

'Isn't your father originally from this area? I wondered if your parents might want to move back.'

'I think Dad might be tempted, but my mother is horrified at the very idea.' Lal smiled at the thought, her face lighting up in a way that intrigued Iain.

'I thought young Bel was planning to stay and live here, won't that be an attraction for your mother?'

Lally pulled a face. 'Bel is only fourteen, far too young to be moving somewhere so remote. It's just a mad idea of hers, she'll get over it.'

'She doesn't think so.' Iain couldn't help smiling as he remembered the girl's enthusiasm. She had explained to him all about home-schooling and assured him that his IT knowledge was coming in extremely handy for organising computer access. 'I'm sure I was never as organised as that at her age.'

'I don't think I'll ever be as organised as that,' said Lal with a sigh. 'But I'm not sure staying here is the right thing for her. And Mum and Dad are absolutely appalled at the idea.'

'She really has thought it all out on her own then?'

'Yes. Unfortunately. I thought it was a passing whim and didn't try too hard to dissuade her at the beginning. That was definitely a mistake. Once she's got the bit between her teeth it's very hard to stop Bel.'

Iain had to concentrate on a difficult manoeuvre passing a campervan that was far too big for these roads. Once that was over he said, 'Wouldn't she be a bit lonely out here? It seems an odd choice for a teenager.'

He could almost feel Lally's mood darken and glanced at her in surprise. He wished this road didn't take so much of his attention.

'She seems to hate school,' said Lally. And then, after a pause and a long sigh, 'She was being bullied.'

'What! But surely . . . ' Iain was about to protest that with her confidence and cheerful personality Bel was the very last person he would expect to suffer from bullying. Then he remembered he had never seen her with other young people. How she had actually seemed afraid of joining the youths on the beach.

'Hard to believe, isn't it?' said Lal bitterly. 'That's why none of us realised. And even now, when I've tried to talk to Mum about it, she seems to think it is something that can be sorted out just like that. We have all of us really let Bel down.'

'Gosh.' Iain drove the remaining distance to Inverloch in silence, shocked by the thoughts that were tumbling into his head. Poor child, so worthwhile but so different, it was easy to see how she might not fit in with other teenagers. It was so unfair. Unlike his popular older brother, Iain had always been a loner himself. He had never actually been bullied, but was aware that in other circumstances it could have happened. This was all wrong. It shouldn't be allowed.

'Here we are,' said Lal, interrupting his thoughts in a falsely cheery tone. 'I usually park in that area facing the sea loch, it's handy for all the shops, but maybe you've found somewhere better yourself?'

'No, here's fine.' Iain swung the car into a free space. He looked out at the view that faced him, the wide greeny-blue loch and the tree-covered hills on the far side, and tried to clear his mind. 'Imagine putting a car park in such a beautiful place,' he said. 'In London and Edinburgh it would be hidden away down some side road.'

'It doesn't make for the prettiest waterfront,' said Lally, collecting together her bags. 'But it is practical and the tourists like it. You'd be amazed how many just come and sit here in their cars, admiring the view, but never actually getting out. But each to their own, I suppose.'

Iain would have quite liked to wander around the shops with Lally, to talk to her some more about Bel (and herself), but she insisted she didn't want to get in his way and headed off to do her own chores. At least he managed to arrange that they meet up in the tiny coffee shop, so he could treat her to a drink and stretch out this time together.

Inverloch was a funny little town. The main street ran along the side of the sea loch, with a mixture of houses, holiday businesses and shops all jumbled together. It seemed a strange arrangement to Iain's city eyes. There was a reasonably well-stocked Spar, and he went here to get the food shopping out of the way first. He'd expected that Lally would be heading here, too, but she had disappeared up one of the side roads. If he had time, after he had done what needed doing, maybe he'd take a wander and see what was so interesting.

But first he had to face Jimmy Jones in the builders' yard and make a decision about what to do with the part of his inheritance that still lay in storage there. He didn't know why this was taking him so long.

The stocky man shook Iain's hand and, once again, chatted for rather longer than Iain would have liked about the weather, and the tides, and something about traffic Iain didn't quite follow. Then he said, 'You'll have phoned the McMichaels about taking on the work for you then?'

'Er, well, not exactly. I still haven't quite decided . . . ' Iain had the phone numbers safely recorded on his phone, but he hadn't been able to bring himself to use them. It was a strange position for him to be in. He was never indecisive. But then he'd never had such a big decision thrust upon him. Choosing which flat to rent in London and now Edinburgh just didn't compare.

'I'll be charging you rental if you leave your things here much longer,' said Jimmy, nodding his head.

Iain had no idea if the man was joking or not. 'Of course. I'm really sorry to impose on you like this . . . '

Now the older man gave a bark of laughter and patted Iain on the arm. 'Dinae worry. I'm no exactly struggling for space, am I now?' He gestured around the yard which was, in fact, half empty. 'I just know Sandy would like to see you getting on with the job, specially with the fine weather we've been having. I've mentioned you to the McMichaels so they'll know what it's about when you phone.'

'Thanks. I'll let you know what I'm going to do shortly. Really, I will.' Iain was glad to get away.

He called in at the Post Office, to send a post-card to his mother who liked that kind of thing, and then made his way to the café. He was early, but had only been perusing the rather short menu for a minute or two when Lally arrived. She was heavily laden and after a laughing conversation with the owner, who she clearly knew, stashed her bags out of the way and came to sit down.

'Did you get everything done you wanted? I hope you haven't had to rush, I'm quite happy to wait.'

'No, that's fine, all done.' Lally took the pale, heavy hair in her hands and lifted it from the back of her neck. 'Phew, it's a bit too hot to be carrying around all the stuff that Gran asked me to pick up. I hope you'll have enough room for it in the car.'

'It's rather a big car.'

'It is, isn't it?' Lally grinned. 'I must admit, I thought it was a bit over the top when I first saw it, but it has its uses.'

'What on earth have you been buying?'

'Oh, not buying. Gran doesn't do buying if she can possibly help it. She's very into bartering. And, unfortunately for you and me, a friend of hers has more tomato and courgette plants than she knows what to do with, plus a sack of last year's carrots that will do for Hamish's pig. Nothing goes to waste if Gran can help it.'

'You shouldn't have carried all that! I could have picked it up in the car for you.'

'If I'd known how much stuff there was I might have asked you to! But never mind, you can help me carry it over from here. Now, what are we having to drink? And eat? Norma makes the most amazing chocolate cake, you'll have to try it.'

Iain, who couldn't remember when he had last had coffee and cake in a café, found he was thoroughly enjoying himself. True, he had to share Lally with half the other visitors, who seemed to know her well and needed to catch up on all the Strathan news, but even that was quite interesting. He learnt that the local primary school was to have two new pupils for the coming term which would take the school roll to fourteen! And that a meeting of Lally's history club had taken place a few days previously. He wished he had known about it.

'How did you get on with your own shopping?' asked Lally, when she was able to return her attention to him. 'At least you weren't in any danger of getting lost in a place this size.'

'Fine. I got everything I needed.' Iain hesitated, and then continued, 'I spent a fair amount of time with Jimmy Jones at the builders' yard. You know Sandy had ordered a whole lot of building material from him?'

'Yes. Sandy was very hot on using local suppliers whenever he could. He and Jimmy got on fine.'

'I don't mean just the things Sandy had used already. There is a whole lot of stuff there he'd ordered, but never even had delivered. He obviously had great plans for the main house, re-roofing it and so on. Everything is just sitting there in the yard, ready to go.'

'Ah,' said Lally, examining him more closely. 'You don't look too happy about that.'

Iain raised his hands in a gesture of defeat. Now he had started on the subject, he was quite keen to continue with it. 'What am I supposed to do? I don't have the skills Great Uncle Alex had.'

'Get someone in to do the work for you then,' said Lally, as though this was obvious. 'There are a couple of local building firms, but the McMichael brothers are said to be the best.'

Iain was beginning to feel there was a conspiracy to get him to commit to doing building work at Harbour House.

'My plan was actually just to put the place on the market,' he said.

'I thought you said you hadn't decided?' said Lally. 'In any case, it would sell better if the house was wind and water-tight, wouldn't it?'

'I suppose it would.'

'And doing that doesn't commit you to Harbour House long term, does it?'

'I suppose not.'

'So, it's obvious. That's what you should do.' Lally grinned at him. She was being very encouraging, almost as if she wanted him to keep the place. That gave him a warm feeling.

She put the last forkful of cake into her mouth and sighed with quite unladylike enjoyment. Then she sat forward and fixed him with a serious stare. 'You know, I've been thinking about this a lot. Maybe there was a special reason why Sandy left Harbour House to you. Family must have been important to him, mustn't it?'

Iain shrugged uncomfortably, remembering his father's story of disagreements never resolved. 'I still think it was probably just a crazy whim.'

'No, Sandy didn't do things on a whim. He must have had a reason. We just need to work out what it was.'

'We do?' Iain meant his tone to be

jokey, but it came out as annoyed. This really wasn't the way he had meant the conversation to go. He wanted to get to know more about Lally, not talk about himself, or his Great Uncle Alex, which he had an uncomfortable feeling would also end up involving talking about himself.

He was thankful to notice a couple hovering in the doorway of the café, looking for an empty table. 'Perhaps we should make a move?' he said. With a bit of luck, by the time they had stowed all Lally's new acquisitions in the car, she would have forgotten this train of thought.

★　★　★

Lally wondered why Iain never wanted to talk about his family or the reasons for his inheritance. She was fascinated by it.

She rather suspected Gran knew more of Sandy's thinking than she was letting on. Iain, on the other hand, seemed to know nothing at all. Wasn't he even interested?

She tried to return to the subject on the journey home, but he only answered in murmurs, pretending to be preoccupied by the road, which couldn't be the case, he'd been happy enough to talk on the way there.

'I can't believe you'd never met Sandy.'

A grunt as he pulled into a passing place to let an approaching car by.

'Didn't he leave you a letter or anything, along with the house? That's what they do in books, isn't it?'

'No, nothing.'

'Don't your parents want to come up and see the place for themselves? Sandy was your dad's uncle, wasn't he? He must remember him at least.'

'Yes, possibly. I have mentioned it to them, but they're a little busy at the moment.'

She was trying to think of some way to get a proper answer out of him when her mobile rang. It was so unexpected, there weren't many stretches of this road where you could get reception, that for a moment she didn't realise what it was.

'It's your phone,' said Iain. 'I'll stop here so you don't get cut off.'

He drew into a viewing place while Lally scrambled in her handbag to find the blessed phone. At last, when she was sure the caller was going to ring off it was taking so long, she pressed the button and held the little machine to her ear.

'Hi there. Yes, this is Lal. Mike! Gosh, I thought it might be my gran asking me to pick up something she had forgotten.'

She smiled apologetically at Iain, who turned to look out of the window so he could pretend he wasn't listening.

Then Mike said something that got her full attention. Something about a short list and an interview.

'I'm sorry, could you say that again?'

'Sorry to call you on your mobile, but it is rather urgent. The Prof has you on the shortlist for the tutoring post. Human Resources were supposed to have contacted you, but there seems to have been a mix up. The interviews are scheduled for next week, but they don't seem to have let two of the applicants know, including you. Do you think you could get down to Edinburgh for Tuesday?'

Lally felt her heart speed up. An interview, for a job she would probably enjoy very much, even if it was in Edinburgh. 'Of course I can. I'll need to check with Gran, but I can't see any problem with me getting away for a day or two. Do you know what time it is? What will I need to do to prepare?'

The rest of the conversation, over a very crackly line, was taken up with making initial arrangements. Mike promised to phone again to confirm everything, as there might not be time for the letter offering an interview to arrive, then rang off.

Lal snapped her phone shut and stretched back in her seat, for once not taking in the wonderful vista of Monros before her.

'Well,' she said.

'Good news?' said Iain politely. He couldn't have avoided hearing at least some of what she had discussed.

'Amazing! I'm on the shortlist for a job in the History Department at Edinburgh University. I applied ages ago and as I'd heard nothing I'd more or less given up. I'll need to start getting organised, I'll have to have something to say about my thesis, and see if I can stay over at my friend Rosie's, and . . . gosh, this is all so sudden.'

'If you needed a lift down to Edinburgh, I'm driving back myself on Saturday.'

Lal grinned at him. He was a bit prim and proper, but he was very kind. Look at the way he had given her this lift today, and then was offering again. 'I'll probably take my own car, it'll be easier. But thanks for thinking of me.'

'Let me know if you change your mind,' he said, pulling carefully back out onto the narrow road. 'And if you're going to be in Edinburgh for a few days perhaps we could meet up for a drink while you're there? I'd like that.'

Lally wasn't sure she could cope with many more surprises. Iain Cunningham was asking her out for a drink? That wasn't just politeness, that was definitely something more.

She tried to study him out of the corner of her eye, not wanting to stare. His clothes were as pristine and conservative as ever. His expression gave nothing away.

'That's very kind of you,' she said. 'If we exchange mobile numbers I'm sure we can sort something out.' As she said the words she felt a small shiver of excitement, quite unconnected with the thrill about being contacted by the university.

★　★　★

Francie was in the kitchen rinsing the first cut of lettuce from the garden when Bel came bouncing in. The girl was tanned from her long days outdoors and the last of her frailness seemed to have gone.

'Isn't it fun, just the two of us,' Bel said. 'I miss Lally of course, but this is still fun. What shall we have for tea? How about mushroom omelette? Lally doesn't like that so it's a good chance to have it now.'

'Actually, I've invited Hamish to eat with us,' said Francie, feeling unaccountably guilty. 'I haven't seen much of him since I got back . . . ' she tailed off, wondering why she felt the need to explain.

'That's a good idea,' said Bel approvingly. 'I've always liked Hamish. And he's been very helpful to Lal over her history society idea.'

'He has, hasn't he?' agreed Francie, relieved. 'Now he's got over the loss of his mother he's really coming out of himself.'

'His mother died years ago,' said Bel, looking confused.

'Three years ago, which isn't so very long when you're our age. And Hamish likes to take things slowly. It can't have been easy for him to adapt to living alone after looking after his mother for so long.'

'He's a funny man,' said Bel, nodding her young head sagely. 'Imagine never marrying and staying at home to look after your parents. It sounds like something out of a Victorian drama.'

'I don't think it was quite like that. However, as I said, it's nice to see him coming out of his shell. Getting him to take his mother's place on the Hall Committee was a masterstroke. And he's really interested in Lal's society. He said to me how much he looks forward to the meetings.'

'Yes. It's really taken off and now Lal is taking the axe head down to Edinburgh maybe they'll be keen to support her idea of a local museum!'

'Lal's a good girl,' said Francie. 'I hope the Society can carry on without her. If she gets this job, she'll be moving

173

back to Edinburgh. I'll miss her.'

'So will I. But she doesn't like mushrooms, and I love them, so lets make the most of her being away just now. Do you think Hamish would be happy to eat omelette with salad from the garden? I was going to do a special omelette, separating the yolks and the whites and whisking up the whites. What do you think?'

'I see you've got it all planned,' said Francie. 'I'm sure Hamish will be delighted with whatever we provide. And if you're going to take charge of the cooking that gives me time to clean out the hen house before he arrives.'

'I was hoping you would have a little rest, Gran.'

'Young lady, I may be old but I'm still perfectly capable of leading an active life! You and Lal fuss about me too much.'

Francie took herself off to the hen house. She didn't know whether to be touched or infuriated by the way the two girls tried to look after her. They meant well, but they didn't realise how much she loved the active life she had here. It had taken those weeks in Broughty Ferry to make her realise quite how lucky she was. And if she was finding things a little more tiring than usual, it was probably because she had got out of the habit of doing exercise.

Very unusually, Hamish didn't arrive a few minutes after the invited time of six o'clock. By half-past six Francie was beginning to wonder if he had forgotten the invitation, although that would be totally unlike him. She was just about to phone to make sure everything was all right when he called her.

'Francie, I'm sorry, I'm so sorry, I won't be able to come over.' His voice was shaking and Francie felt her heart begin to thud. What could have happened to upset calm and careful Hamish like this?

'What is it? Are you all right?'

She heard him take a deep, shuddering breath. 'I'm fine. It's . . . it's Suzie. She's hurt herself badly. I'll need to take her to the vet.'

Now Francie understood his pain. Since the death of his parents, Suzie, his darling little Jack Russell, had been everything to him.

'Can I help? Should I come over?'

'No. Yes. Yes, if you wouldn't mind. If you could come with me to the vet's, it's such a long way to Inverloch. If you could hold her while I drive. Francie, she's bleeding such a lot. And it was my fault!'

'We'll be right over,' said Francie.

She called Bel to cease her omelette-making preparations, picked up her jacket and handbag, and headed for her car. She explained as much as she knew to Bel as she drove rather more quickly than usual along the winding road.

The journey into Inverloch was a nightmare. Francie took one look at the tiny dog wrapped in a towel but with blood seeping horribly through, and insisted that Hamish hold her whilst Francie drove. The poor little thing was trembling and cowering into her owner.

It was best if the two weren't separated.

Hamish didn't even protest. He just slid into the passenger seat and asked her to drive as fast as she dared. 'The young vet, James, is expecting us. He'll do what he can. We just need to get her there.' Hamish was shaking almost as much as his dog.

Francie decided to save her questions for later and concentrate on the road. Even Bel was silent.

It wasn't a journey Francie ever wanted to repeat. Every corner and bump felt twice as bad as usual. The dog didn't quite whimper, but her rasping breathing would pause, as though she was gathering herself to survive the pain. Hamish told her over and over again she was a good girl, and everything would be all right, and how sorry he was.

Each time Francie glanced sideways the stain of blood on the towel seemed to have grown bigger. Whatever was wrong with the little dog was very serious indeed.

The vet was waiting for them as they pulled up outside his door. He took Suzie from Hamish, shouted something to the nurse who was by his side and the two disappeared.

Francie, Hamish and Bel sat down on the hard plastic chairs of the waiting room, and just looked at each other.

'I'm sure he'll do everything he can,' said Francie gently. She hesitated. 'Do you want to tell us what happened?'

Hamish's curly grey head was drooped so low she could hardly see his expression. He rubbed a shaking hand across his eyes and gave a long sigh. 'I did it. It was my fault. So stupid.'

'I'm sure it wasn't,' said Bel, but Francie shook her head at the girl. Just let him speak.

Hamish continued as though he hadn't heard. 'I was clearing out the old byre, so I was. My father never liked to throw anything out and Mum and I had never got around to sorting it. I'd brought your things over as we discussed a couple of weeks ago, Francie. I thought

178

a nice dry day like today was just the opportunity I needed to sort my own before I called in the scrap metal people. And then I got to wondering if there might not be something of interest in there for Lally. For her Historical Society, you know.

'My father had farming implements going back to the dark ages.' He shot Francie the very faintest smile as he said this. She knew that it was something he had tried, in his quiet way, to do — bring his father's way of caring for the land into the twentieth if not the twenty-first century.

'There were old scythes and ploughs and I don't know what. Very rusted too, I felt ashamed we hadn't taken better care of them. Suzie was around, keeping me company as she always does.' He paused to take a large white handkerchief out of his pocket and blow his nose. 'I told her to keep out from under my feet and I thought she'd maybe gone for a wee sleep in that spot she likes by the back dyke so I wasn't thinking. I'd got onto the upper floor of the byre by then and decided to drop some of the things out of those big double doors straight to the ground outside. I wasn't even looking. So careless of me. It was only when I heard Suzie yelp that I realised . . . I realised I'd dropped an old rashes scythe right on top of her. The end caught her tummy and sliced through . . . I'd no idea something so blunt could do so much damage.'

Francie put her arm around the poor man and gave him an awkward hug. 'Poor poor you, but you mustn't blame yourself. An accident like that could happen to anyone. And perhaps it looks worse than it is.'

'James is a really good vet, I've heard he specialises in surgery, so he's the very best person to have.' Really, Bel was an amazing source of information, Francie didn't know where she picked it all up, but she was pleased to be reminded of this.

'That's right, I'd heard that too. He

and that nice vet nurse will do their very best for her. All we can do is wait, and pray.'

Hamish nodded, but said nothing. Now he had finally told his story he seemed unable to do anything more.

It was Bel who jumped up after five minutes or so. 'What we all need is a nice hot drink. I'm going to go down to the fish and chip shop, I know they do takeaway tea and coffee. What would you prefer? Coffee, and lots of sugar? And if I could borrow some money, Gran?'

She took herself off, her face still troubled, but determined to do what she could to help.

'She's a good girl,' said Francie.

'Aye, she is that. It's a fine idea for her to stay at Strathan.'

Francie was surprised at the comment. She didn't even know Hamish was aware of this possibility, never mind had an opinion on it.

'Why do you say that?' she asked, keen to distract him.

Hamish shook his head, struggling to focus on her. 'It'll be company for you. It's not right living on your own and the child is meant to live out here. A city isn't the right place for her.'

Francie pondered his words, and found herself agreeing with them. 'I'm happy on my own,' she said, protesting as a matter of form, 'But I would enjoy having her to stay longer. I was worried it would be bad for her, to hide away here. If you're right and this is the place that suits her — well, that's different.'

'Aye. It is. Strathan suits some people. Like me. I've never wanted to leave.'

'Nor have I.'

'You're not from Strathan,' said Hamish, looking at her properly for the first time since they had arrived. 'Your family lived the other side of Inverloch. It was Bill who was Strathan born and bred.'

'I still think of myself as local,' said Francie, suppressing a smile. Being born even ten miles from Strathan would make you a foreigner in Hamish's world. Not that he wouldn't welcome you and be perfectly friendly, but you would never quite belong. She sighed. How many true locals would be left here in the years to come? Her own son had moved away, as had almost every other young person in the last half century. Perhaps Bel could be the start of a reverse trend?

The girl herself returned at that moment, her arms full of horrible polystyrene cups. She looked a little flustered, but handed the drinks around and asked politely if there was any news.

Francie told her there was nothing yet and they all settled back down on the uncomfortable chairs. She had to admit, when she took a first sip, that the hot drink had been a very good idea.

She glanced surreptitiously at her watch. How long had they been here? How much longer would they have to wait until they heard news?

★　★　★

Lal was standing on the busy pavement of Princes Street in Edinburgh, wondering how a city she had lived in for five years could suddenly seem so strange. There were too many people, and all in such a hurry. They kept bumping into her, glaring at her for standing still. It was early evening and the place was incredibly busy. She thought of the sunlight glistening off the wide bay of Strathan, and sighed.

She decided to cross the road and sit in the Princes Street Gardens for a little while. She still had fifteen minutes before she was due to meet Iain, and she had an awful lot to get her head around.

She found an empty wooden bench and settled down on it. She could look up at the grey bulk of the castle and the higgledy-piggledy line of old houses along the Royal Mile. Now she was away from the traffic and the people she remembered she did like Edinburgh. It was beautiful, in a totally different way to Strathan.

She tried to picture herself living here once again. It seemed like it might actually happen! Instead of being delighted, she felt merely confused. The interview had gone very well, and although nothing formal had been said she had been given the very clear impression that if she wanted the job it was hers. Mike had primed her with a lot of useful information and it seemed she had said all the right things. So why was she not more excited? It should have been the perfect move.

She sighed and turned away from the skyline to look at the pigeons pecking about her feet. Such busy things, so concentrated on their own business. They reminded her of Bel, engrossed and purposeful, and she felt a pang of longing to see her sister again. Which was ridiculous, she had only been away two days.

She was glad when it was time to leave her thoughts behind and head for the bar on Frederick Street where she had agreed to meet Iain.

He was there before her, as she had hoped he would be. He stood at the steps that led down to the basement bar, looking very smart and business-like in a dark suit and brilliantly white shirt. The tidiness of his casual clothes at Strathan were nothing in comparison to this. Lal immediately wished she was wearing something nicer than the dull brown skirt and cream blouse she had put on for her interview.

He bent and kissed her cheek as if they were old friends. Lal could feel herself blushing.

'Hello there, I hope I haven't kept you waiting . . . '

'Not at all. Let's go and see if we can find a table, shall we?' They descended the narrow stairs to a low-roofed, white-walled room where everything was stylish and angular and Lal felt even more out of place.

Iain found them a corner table and went to buy drinks. He returned with a beer for himself and a white wine spritzer for Lally. She sipped it and surveyed the clientele.

'I don't remember Edinburgh people being so smart when I was living here. Or maybe I just didn't come to places like this.'

Iain looked around, frowning. 'Is this smart? A colleague at work recommended it. It seems all right to me.'

'That's because you're a Londoner. Everywhere is super chic down there, or so I've heard. Next time we go out you should let me take you to one of my old student haunts, that'll show you a different side of the city.' Now where had that suggestion come from? She was heading back to Strathan in a couple of days time so there probably wouldn't be a next time.

'I'll look forward to it,' said Iain, and smiled. When he smiled he looked so different, approachable and actually rather handsome. Lally hadn't been able to see that at first, he had seemed so neat and uptight and really not her kind of person. It was Bel who kept going on about his eyes, so dark with beautiful thick lashes.

Now Lally realised she was staring and looked away.

'How did your interview go?' asked Iain after a pause, as though he too had been distracted.

'Quite well, I think. But I won't know anything for a week or so.'

'It sounds like an excellent job, very good career progression,' said Iain, and Lal could feel her spirits falling.

He was absolutely right, it was a good career move. Her father would be over the moon if she was offered this job. So why wasn't she happier herself?

'It all sounds very positive,' said Iain, encouragingly. Maybe he sensed her doubts. 'The university people obviously think you're something special if they took so much trouble to make sure you didn't miss your interview.'

'They are being very helpful,' said Lally, feeling bad she wasn't more grateful. 'Mike, one of my old lecturers, has offered to meet me for coffee and a chat tomorrow. He's very kind.'

'Unusually so,' said Iain, as though he didn't approve.

'He says this is an ideal opportunity for me to come back to Edinburgh.' Lal wrinkled her nose.

'It sounds like you've got an admirer there,' said Iain, frowning. 'Maybe he's got his own reasons for wanting you to move back?'

'No, no, Mike's just a friend. He's very supportive of lots of his students.' As she said this, Lally wondered how true it was. Mike was being particularly helpful to her. 'Anyway, he's far too old for me. Late thirties at least.'

'And you are?'

'Twenty-three, twenty-four next month.'

'You seem older,' he said, frowning again. 'You've so much confidence.'

Lally shrugged uncomfortably, wondering if her age was an issue for him. 'It's a Dunmore thing, our family all seem to have masses of confidence, but we don't really. Look at Bel, she's bursting with self-assurance most of the time, but we know now there is a problem when she's with other young-sters.' She sighed. 'I wish she hadn't been so good at hiding that from us.'

They moved on to discussing Bel and the issue of age was forgotten. It was only later that Lally wished she had asked Iain how old he was. Around thirty, she would have guessed. Initially his rather prim attitude had made him seem far older, but now he was beginning to relax she decided he was definitely a lot younger than Mike.

★　★　★

The vet had finally come out to give them some news. He was holding a towel on which he was still drying his hands, and looked rather pale and tense, but he said the operation had gone as well as could be expected and now they just needed to wait and see how the wee dog progressed.

'But you think . . . ' Hamish coughed and cleared his throat. 'But you do think she will pull through?'

'I think she has every chance,' said the young vet, but his expression was still serious. 'She'd lost a lot of blood and it was a deep and rather dirty cut, but I think we've cleaned it all out. I've stitched her up and started her on antibiotics so I'm hopeful we'll avoid any infection.'

'Thank you,' said Hamish, still with a catch in his voice. 'Thank you so much. Do anything you can, I'm not worried about the cost, just as long as you can save Suzie.'

James nodded his understanding. Then he offered to take Hamish through to see the little dog and for a moment Francie and Bel were left alone in the waiting room.

'Do you think she'll survive?' asked Bel in a whisper. 'James didn't seem all that certain.'

'He's done what he can. And Suzie is a tough wee thing, a fighter, if any dog can come through she can.'

'I hope so. Hamish will be really upset if she doesn't.'

Francie didn't even want to think about that possibility. She rubbed her hands together. They were getting rather cold from sitting so long. It was time to move, to think of something more positive.

'Why don't we take Hamish out for a meal? I don't think he's going to want to be too far from Suzie and it'll be something to pass the time.'

'Oh, yes, excellent idea. Too bad about my mushroom omelette, but we can have that some other time. I haven't been to the Clachan Arms for ages. Do they still do that brilliant mussel soup?'

Francie was glad that Bel, at least, could be so easily distracted. Hamish wasn't actually keen to leave the vet's surgery, but James insisted there was nothing more they could do until Suzie came round from the anaesthetic, so eventually he allowed himself to be led away.

The Clachan Arms was on a corner a few minutes' walk from the surgery. They had to pass the fish and chip shop where Bel had been to buy the coffee. Bel was walking slightly ahead of them and Francie noticed her granddaughter shy away from the group of youngsters who were standing around the open doorway.

One of the boys noticed her and called, 'So you're back? Why'd you no' say hello before?'

Bel held her head high and ignored him.

Francie was sure the youth meant no harm, it was just teenage high spirits, showing off in front of his friends, but the way Bel reacted seemed to encourage him to tease her more. He had taken a step towards her before he saw the adults and stopped. Bel looked petrified. Francie wondered what would have happened if she and Hamish hadn't been there.

Hamish seemed to have missed the interlude between Bel and the boy entirely. He now came to himself and noticed the youth. 'Oh, it's yourself, Lachy Kirkpatrick,' he said. 'Does your mother know you're in the town?'

The boy's cocky attitude disintegrated immediately. 'Aye, aye, she knows fine,' he said, his head drooping.

'Well, if you want a lift back along the road you can give us a wee shout later on. We'll be here until at least eleven, I need to check on my dog at the vet's.'

'Is Suzie no' well?' asked the youth, his voice filled now with nothing but concern. He was a nice boy, after all. Francie thought she recognised him from Clashnessie, the village half-way between Strathan and Inverloch. Hamish, of course, knew everyone for miles around.

Hamish explained what had happened to his little dog and all the youngsters crowded round to hear, expressing their shock and sympathy with *oohs* and *aahs*. Bel stayed on the other side of her gran, but Francie hoped she realised there was a good side to these youngsters and that she didn't need to be so wary of them.

She tried to find a way of saying this as they headed into the hotel, but Bel seemed determined to change the subject and for the moment Francie let it go.

After they had eaten they returned to the vet's surgery and were delighted to hear that Suzie had come round from the anaesthetic and was already starting to take an interest in her surroundings. The vet had every hope that she would now make a good recovery.

★ ★ ★

Iain went back to his flat after meeting with Lally and wondered what was wrong. He looked around and realised everything seemed so dull. Lally wasn't dull, and nor was her grandmother, Francie, or her strange little sister, Bel. They all had such an enthusiasm for life, which he found it hard to muster as he sat there.

He looked around the apartment again, and thought of the Bothy, and it occurred to him he would far rather be there. He could be sitting in the long, light room, with the view of the sea before him. It would still be light there, it was so far north, although it was now after eleven. He wondered what it would be like to live there permanently. Which was impossible, of course. He didn't know why he had even thought of it.

The most he could hope for was that Lally would get the job in Edinburgh, and she would bring some of that enthusiasm for life down here with her. He would definitely make sure he saw more of her.

Then he remembered all the work he had to do, and turned his computer on, and made himself concentrate on that.

Bel Makes A Breakthrough

Lal had one more thing to do before she returned to Strathan. The little box containing the axe head was hidden safely in the depths of her bulky shoulder bag. She was to take it to the museum.

She felt guilty and excited. The guilt was because she knew the find should have been declared long ago and she was worried about how best to stop Arthur getting into trouble. He might be pedantic and annoying, but he had finally seen sense. The excitement was because this might be a very important find. She would know the truth soon.

She had made an appointment to see a woman called Lucinda Hayes who was a member of the Treasure Trove team. Despite having worked in the museum herself, Lal had had nothing to do with that department and didn't know what to expect.

She made her way to the designated area and gave in her name, trying to sound calm and composed when she was shaking with nerves. She wished she had put on something smarter than jeans and a multi-coloured woollen jacket. She really needed this woman to take her seriously. Oh why didn't she hurry up and appear? The wait was making Lal doubt herself even more. Ah, here she was.

Lucinda Hayes proved to be a slight, angular woman in her late fifties. Her approach was no nonsense and to the point.

'You have something you want to show me? Normally we prefer people to fill in forms and go through the proper channels.'

'I'm sorry. I thought you'd probably want to see this as soon as possible.' Lal carefully removed the lid of the box and handed it over. 'This was found on a hillside in north west Sutherland. I think it's a ceremonial . . . '

'Quiet,' said the woman, taking the box reverently in her hands and turning it round and round. To Lal, it felt as though time stood still. The woman was obviously thrilled. Colour had come into her pale cheeks and she reached for gloves to put on before handling the stone. If you weren't interested in history, especially ancient history, you probably wouldn't understand this emotion. Lal did.

'Am I right? Is it special?' she asked, when she could bear to wait no longer.

The woman made an impatient gesture and continued with her examination. She was now using a magnifying glass to study the dark shiny object from all angles.

Eventually she put it down and said, 'Well, this is rather interesting. Sutherland, you say? Can you tell me exactly when and where it was found?'

Lal launched into her pre-prepared speech, about how the man who had found it a couple of years previously hadn't realised what it was and how the establishment of the local historical society had brought it to her attention. She had gleaned as much information as she could from Arthur and had even gone up the hillside herself and taken some photographs which she was able to pass on to Lucinda.

'This is a rare and remarkable item,' said the older woman, her eyes glistening. 'I will, of course, have to verify various things and discuss it with my colleagues, but I think I can say the ramifications of the find are significant. Previously there has been no proof that these axes were traded so far afield. And if this really is a ceremonial axe, that tells us all sorts of things about how developed the local culture was. Oh, this is so exciting!'

Lal let out a long breath. It was going brilliantly. The find was just as important as she suspected, and with a bit of luck neither she nor Arthur were going to get into too much trouble. Lucinda was far too pleased to have the artefact in her hands to worry about the minutiae of Treasure Trove laws.

Lucinda became almost chatty, gloating over the little piece of stone, musing about the possibility of arranging a dig in the area to see if they could find other treasures.

After the very successful visit to the museum, Lal went to meet Mike.

He knew the purpose of her meeting with Lucinda Hayes and was delighted it had gone so well. 'I told you not to worry,' he said rather smugly, although Lally remembered he had been most disapproving that the find hadn't been handed in sooner.

'It's brilliant,' she said. 'Hopefully this will make them take the history of the north of Scotland much more seriously. It's exactly what the area needs.'

'Although you may well not be living there much longer,' said Mike, smiling at her. 'I can't say anything officially, of course, but I'm hoping you'll hear about how your interview went very soon. And I can say that I for one would be delighted to have you back in Edinburgh.'

'Thank you, that's very kind.' Lal began to feel a little uncomfortable. Until Iain had put the idea into her head, she had never thought Mike considered her anything more than a protégée. Now she wondered if he might be interested in her romantically. That really wasn't what she wanted. She glanced across at him and saw he was watching her closely.

'I'm not being kind,' he said. 'I'm hoping that you and I can spend more time together when you move back. In fact, if you're staying for a few more days just now, why don't we try and fit in a trip to the theatre?'

Yes, that was it. There was no doubt about it. He was asking her out. Lal hoped she wasn't blushing.

'That's very kind,' she said again. 'However, I'm heading over to see my parents first thing tomorrow and then back to Strathan. And actually, I'm not that keen on the theatre.'

'Ah. Perhaps we could go to a film, or as you young people call it, a movie, once you are back?'

'Perhaps,' said Lal, smiling and trying desperately to think how she could tell him she wasn't interested and yet not hurt him. She liked Mike and he had always been a great help to her, but as a boyfriend? Oh no. Iain Cunningham on the other hand, she could very easily consider in that light . . .

Which gave her just the idea she needed. 'It would be fun if a few of us went out together. My friend, Iain, and Rosie who I'm staying with. Of course, I don't know when I'll be back in Edinburgh, but I'll bear it in mind.'

After that the conversation turned to less troubling things. Lal still felt Mike looking at her rather more lingeringly than she would have liked, but she hoped he had got the message.

* * *

It was the day for Suzie to have her stitches out and Hamish had invited the Dunmores around for a cup of tea to celebrate her recovery. Once she turned the corner, the little dog had healed remarkably quickly. After a worrying first couple of days she had come on in leaps and bounds. Hamish had insisted on taking her home and nursing her himself, and he had certainly done a good job.

Now, with the stitches out and the plastic collar removed from her head, she looked almost like her old self. If you ignored the shaven patch on her side. And the fact she was no longer the rather solid little terrier of old, but slimmer and possibly greyer.

Lal was delighted to see her, and to see Hamish looking so happy and relaxed once more. He fussed around them, making sure they were sitting comfortably in the neat and tidy sitting room that was such a contrast to the messy working croft outside.

'I'd forgotten how lovely the views

are from here,' said Lal to her gran, whilst Hamish went off to fetch the tea and biscuits. Bel bounced back out of her chair to help him.

'Yes. I've been telling Hamish he should really change the house around, make more use of this room by converting it to a kitchen-cum-dining room. He spends far more time in the kitchen than in here and it's such a waste.'

'But this was his mother's favourite room,' said Lal, shocked.

'Yes. And see how he hasn't changed a thing.' Francie shook her head, looking worried. 'I thought he was moving on, but if he can't alter the house to suit his way of living then he isn't.'

'He has changed in some ways,' said Lal, thinking of how positive he had been about the Historical Society.

'I thought so,' said Francie, looking unexpectedly gloomy. 'When I was away looking after Bridget he seemed different, but now I'm home . . . '

Whatever she had been about to say was cut off by the return of the others with the trays.

It was a pleasant, relaxing afternoon. They chatted as only good friends could, and Gran seemed to cheer up and forget her worry that Hamish wasn't 'moving on'. Suzie sat quietly at Hamish's feet, accepting the occasional tidbit from him. Actually, now Lal came to think of it, the little terrier looked rather smug. She was enjoying all the attention!

The Dunmores were just thinking about leaving when there was a knock on the front door.

'Goodness,' said Hamish. 'More visitors.'

'I'll go and see who it is,' said Bel, jumping up and bustling out. 'Probably one of your neighbours wanting to see how Suzie is . . . oh.'

Her voice tailed off and Lal, Gran and Hamish looked at each other, wondering what could have stopped Bel in full flow.

Hamish rose to his feet and at the same time Bel led the new arrivals into the sitting room. She hurried back to her own seat. 'People to see you,' she muttered.

'We came to see how wee Suzie is doing, I hope you don't mind?'

Lal recognised the girl from the Historical Society, she was one of the two teenagers who had continued to attend the meetings, despite Bel's expectations. She thought the girl lived at Clashnessie and was called either Isla or Morag, she could never tell the two girls apart. She had a boy with her, who could only have been her brother.

'Morag, well this is a nice surprise,' said Hamish, immediately becoming the good host. 'And Lachy too. Take a wee seat and I'll put the kettle on.'

'You don't need to do that,' said the girl. 'We can't stay long. I'm giving Lachy a lift to go surfing in Strathan Bay. Did you know I passed my driving test last week? But Lachy has been telling us what a bad accident Suzie had and we wanted to come in and see her, see how she's doing.'

'We brought her this,' said the boy. He had the same dark hair as his sister, although his was curly. And he had a very spotty face, but Lal noticed the nice smile as he handed over a packet of dog chews.

Suzie had been watching the visitors balefully from her master's feet, but now decided it was worth her while to greet them. She rose stiffly (Lal rather thought she was putting it on) and tottered over.

'You wee darling, how are you doing?' Morag fell to her knees and stroked Suzie under her grey and white muzzle. Suzie put up with this patiently, her eyes all the while on the packet of treats.

'This is very kind of you,' said Hamish. 'Are you sure you'll not stay for a drink?'

'We need to go or we'll miss the tide,' said Lachy.

His sister sighed. 'I'm just the

chauffeur. I don't know why I was so keen to get my licence, now he expects me to drive him everywhere.'

'You offered.'

Lachy seemed to be a boy of few words, at least in this company. He edged towards the door, clearly willing his sister to hurry up.

'I don't know what I'm going to do whilst he's surfing,' Morag continued happily. 'I meant to bring a book along, but I forgot. I don't suppose you, Bel — it is Bel, isn't it? Would you like to come with us? You and I could walk out to the archway whilst he surfs, I haven't done that walk for ages.'

Bel looked stunned at the suggestion. Lal and Gran both jumped in at the same time.

'That's an excellent idea!'

'You love that walk, Bel. Off you go.'

'I'd really appreciate the company,' continued Morag chattily. 'And you can tell me what was discussed at the last Historical Society meeting, would you mind? I was really annoyed to miss it.'

Lal watched her sister, willing her to agree. Morag was a nice girl. She remembered her better now, she was the more chatty of the two girls, always interested and friendly.

So far Lal didn't think Bel had said a word directly to Morag or Isla and had always made sure she sat as far from them as possible. Which was ridiculous. Not all youngsters were horrible. She had to realise that.

'Oh, for goodness sake, come on,' said Lachy, and somehow it was his impatience that decided Bel.

She jumped up guiltily. 'Sorry, I didn't mean to keep you back.'

'You're coming? Brill, let's go then.' Morag raised a hand in a cheery fare-well to the adults and the three youngsters departed.

'Do you think she'll be all right?' said Lally, worried now.

'Aye, she'll be fine,' said Hamish. 'The Kirkpatricks are a nice family. It's good for Bel to start mixing.'

* * *

Lal had come to a decision. Unfortunately, it wasn't a popular one. She had been offered the job at the university, and she had turned it down. It just didn't feel right, and after discussing it with Gran she realised that if something felt wrong, it was wrong.

Sadly, not everyone was able to see things this way. Mike was most put out, but Lal's real worry was her parents. For the first time in her life, she found herself at loggerheads with them.

They were very disappointed about the job. They also seemed to be holding her responsible for Bel's continued desire to move permanently to Strathan.

They were on the phone once again to make this very point.

'The more we think about it, the more we think Bel should come home now,' said her mother. 'The longer she stays there, the harder it is going to be for her to see sense. Now your gran is back you don't need Bel there to keep you company. In fact, Lal, I really don't think you need to be at Strathan either. It was supposed to be a little break, doing Gran a favour. We didn't expect you to disappear never to return.'

'I haven't disappeared! And I probably will come back, I do realise I need to find work, but I'm enjoying the summer up here, Mum. I didn't want to commit to the job in Edinburgh, they really wanted someone who would join the department long term and I didn't feel I could promise that.'

'It would have been an excellent career opportunity, according to your father. You need to start being serious about life, Alicia. You can't expect things to just happen, you need to plan for them.

'Now can I have a word with Bel? Anthony is arriving home at the weekend and we thought we could bring him up for a visit and then Bel can come back with us.'

'Mum, I'm not sure . . . '

'We've spoken to the school about

the, er, bullying. They've agreed to look into things. We'll get it sorted out. Now put Bel on the phone, will you, and I'll tell her so herself?'

Reluctantly Lal did as requested. Her heart sank as she saw the grim expression on her little sister's face. Bel didn't argue with her mother, she just refused to discuss her return to Glasgow.

After the call, she took herself off to the bay on her own. Lal sighed. The child had seemed so happy lately, had even spent a couple of afternoons on the beach with Morag and her brother and seemed far less wary of them than she had done. Lal was beginning to think moving here might really be the right answer for her sister. How could she get her parents to see that?

Later that afternoon, the phone rang again. Gran answered it as she came in from the garden, her hands soil-covered as she never did remember to wear her gardening gloves.

'It's for you, Lal,' she said, handing

over the receiver after brushing the dirt off it. 'It's Anka. I can't think why she wants to speak to you, but she was most insistent.'

Anka spoke in her usual brisk way. 'I hear you continue to stay at Strathan, yes?'

'For the moment, yes.'

'I need to return to Norway for some weeks. My mother has been unwell and now she is to have an operation. I am thinking perhaps you could look after Achmore for me? There are not many people I could trust, but you did a good job at Tigh na Mara and I trust you.'

'Gosh,' said Lal, momentarily speechless, both at Anka's suggestion and the unexpected compliment. 'Er, if you need someone, I'd be delighted to help.'

'Good. I will of course pay. Why you don't come over tomorrow and we can discuss?'

This was agreed and Lal hurried out to give her news to Gran, who was hoeing the lazy beds.

'A job! I've got a job. I know it's only

for a few weeks, but she says she'll pay me. And I can stay in Strathan. Aren't I lucky?'

'Anka will be very lucky to have you,' said Gran.

'I hope I manage OK. This is such good news, now Mum and Dad can't say I'm wasting my time staying up here.' Lal smiled at the thought that sometimes things did just happen, despite what her parents said.

'We know that time at Strathan is never wasted. Bel and I will miss you, although Achmore is only down the road.'

'If I'm still here,' said Bel. She was standing at the corner of the house, watching them but not joining in. 'Mum and Dad can't stop you staying, but what about me?'

Lal and Gran both opened their mouths, looking for the right thing to say, but before either of them had found it Bel had heaved a massive sigh and disappeared once more.

A Decision Is Made

Iain was very disappointed when he learnt Lal had turned down the job in Edinburgh. It made him realise how much he had counted on her moving closer. He found himself using any excuse to contact her.

First it was to check on how Hamish's little dog was doing, then to offer the loan of the Bothy for when her parents visited. Another excuse came when his own parents announced they had cleared some time in their diaries to make a visit to Harbour House.

Iain had begun to think they weren't ever going to visit, and wondered if that might not be a good thing. Was there really any need to delve into the past? But now they had decided to come he felt he could at least use this as a reason to phone Tigh na Mara.

The first thing he asked about was

the job-hunting. He was still hopeful that her search would bring her back to Edinburgh.

'Actually, I'm going to be doing some work on a neighbour's croft,' she said, sounding delighted.

'Oh. That's good.' Iain tried to hide his disappointment. 'I still think it's a shame you turned down that post at the university.' He knew it was none of his business, but nevertheless, he found it hard to understand.

'It just didn't feel right.' Lally sighed. 'Everyone thinks I'm mad, especially my parents. And Mike, my old lecturer, is really upset. I think he'd really supported my application which makes me feel bad.'

Iain remembered he had already taken a dislike to this unknown Mike. 'You don't need to feel bad. If it's not the right job for you, then it isn't. Something else will turn up.'

He didn't know where that phrase came from. It wasn't the usual sort of thing he said. He was all for careful planning, not taking a leap into the unknown.

'Yes, and now this work for Anka has! Gran and Bel are really pleased, they're the only ones who haven't said I'm being stupid.'

'Of course you're not being stupid,' said Iain, wanting more than ever to see her, to cheer her up.

He remembered the reason for this call and told her of his parents' intended visit at the end of August.

As he had hoped, she was immediately enthusiastic. 'That would be great. I'm sure they'll love this place. And then you would really be able to talk to them about Sandy, find out what they know.'

'Mmm,' said Iain, remembering his doubts about digging into the past. 'Of course it's really good that they're visiting, although I don't know where we'll all stay. The Bothy isn't exactly spacious, which is why I'm phoning. I wondered if you knew of some suitable accommodation nearby.'

'Let your parents have the Bothy,'

said Lally immediately. 'You can stay with us at Gran's.'

'I couldn't do that. You don't really have much space, do you? No, that's not . . .'

'It'll be fine. In fact, I might still be staying at Achmore. You're lending us the Bothy when my parents visit. Then we can help you out later when your parents come up. That's what neighbours do.'

Before he could protest further, he heard Lally calling out to her gran who apparently thought the invitation a wonderful idea.

'Gran says that'll be fine. You should have realised by now how hospitable she is.'

'Thank you, that's really very kind of you all, but that wasn't what I expected when I phoned for advice.'

'We know that. Don't worry about it. We'll look forward to seeing you, and Gran will be interested to meet your parents. She's been wondering about them for ages.'

'I'm sure they'll be delighted to meet

her, too,' said Iain politely, his happiness at the thought of seeing Lal again now tempered with concern about what Francie Dunmore might say to his parents.

As far as he could remember they liked intrusive people even less than Iain himself. He'd have to try and explain about Highland hospitality, and how it wasn't really nosiness when they asked all those questions. He wasn't at all certain his parents would understand.

After that phone call he pondered for a few minutes on his parents, and the Dunmores, and Strathan. Then he decided.

He searched on his mobile for the number he had been given all those weeks ago: the building brothers, the McMichaels. It was about time he did something about Harbour House.

★ ★ ★

Francie was worried about Bel. Since that last phone call from her parents she had withdrawn into herself. When asked if there was anything she wanted to talk about, she denied it, although Francie could tell she was brooding. This was so unlike the normal sunny, chatty Bel and it made Francie very concerned.

Like Bel's parents, Francie had found it hard to believe the child had really been bullied. In fact, she had half suspected a genuine love of Strathan had put Bel up to the idea of relocating there rather than a problem at school. Now she was starting to think differently. Bel was far too wary around other young people. The budding friendship between Bel and Morag and Lachy Kirkpatrick seemed to have ground to a halt too.

Francie couldn't discuss this with Lal, who she knew was as worried as she was, and also now frantically busy learning how to milk goats and do all the other chores Anka insisted were necessary. It therefore seemed obvious to turn to Hamish. She would drive over to his croft and have a chat with him, see if Suzie was continuing her excellent recovery. That was a perfectly good reason for visiting, wasn't it?

She found Hamish in the field across the road from his house, shearing sheep with a hand clipper. He had set up a little pen and had a good system going, but nevertheless it looked like hard work.

Most of the crofters still sheared this way, not having enough animals to make it worthwhile bringing in a contractor. Really, it wasn't surprising so few young people were keen to take on this way of life.

Hamish seemed pleased to see her, or pleased to have an excuse to down tools for a while. He released the latest sheep and the animal lumbered away, looking thin and vulnerable without her woolly coat.

He wiped his forehead with the back of his hand. His curls were damp. 'Phew, I'm glad I'm nearly through this lot. Have you time for a quick cup of tea? I'd fair welcome a break.'

Francie agreed and they crossed the narrow road back to the house. She paused, looking around. Something was different, which she hadn't noticed when she had parked the car.

'You've got rid of all the old machinery!'

'Aye. You could say, about time too. The scrap man came round last Friday and gave me a quote. It wasn't a lot of money, but I was glad to be shot of the stuff, especially after Suzie's little accident.' He shuddered and stooped to pat the terrier who was following at his heel. 'I've kept some of the really old things in case Lal ever gets her museum off the ground. He came and collected the rest yesterday. I was going to phone you about your share of the money.'

'I don't want anything, I was just grateful to you for taking it away for me.' Francie shuddered too. She couldn't help thinking she was partly to blame for Suzie's mishap. It had been her request to Hamish that had spurred him on to clear out his barns.

'I'll make sure you get your fair share,' said Hamish, so firmly she decided not to argue with him just now.

They went through to the little kitchen and set out the tea things between them. Hamish was an easy companion, he neither objected to her help nor expected her to do everything for him.

'Let's sit outside,' said Francie. 'It's cleared up beautifully after last night's storm, but I'm not sure how many good days we have left this summer.'

'We have to make the most of what we get,' agreed Hamish, and they went to sit on the garden bench that had stood beside the front door for as long as Francie could remember. Not that Hamish's mother had ever actually sat on it, she hadn't liked to be outside much.

Francie told Hamish about Lal looking after the croft for Anka. This made her think of Iain Cunningham, who was planning another visit soon.

She was quietly hopeful Iain was getting attached to Harbour House and would keep it, as Sandy had wanted. 'It would be ideal if he moved out here to live permanently. I'm sure he could do his IT work from wherever he wanted, if he put his mind to it.'

'That's a big step for a townie like him.'

'It would be good, though. And then he and Lally could get together and she would stay here too.

Hamish smiled. 'Aye, that would be fine. I see you've got it all worked out. They're getting friendly, are they?'

'Not as much as I would like.' Francie sighed. 'I can see they're interested in each other, but neither of them seems willing to make the first move. I don't know why.'

'Not everyone is so keen to take the bull by the horns as you are.'

'I know.' Francie sighed again.

'Give them time,' said Hamish. He had never been one to hurry things and Francie smiled and relaxed, pleased she had come to visit. He was a good person to be around.

She took a deep breath and moved onto the subject of Bel, the real reason for the visit. 'Peter and his wife want Bel to go back to Glasgow, they're talking about coming to collect her this weekend.'

'Oh,' said Hamish. He understood immediately this wasn't good. 'Have you tried talking to them?'

'Lally and I both have, but for some reason they're not prepared to listen. I think they don't really believe the bullying was serious, despite anything we say. And she is their daughter, I can't keep her here against their wishes. I'm worried they think I'm encouraging her to stay here. Of course, I'd love the company, but that's not why I agreed. I just want to do what is best, but how do I know what that is? And if staying here is the right thing, how do I persuade Peter and Sally?'

'Let's take this one step at a time,' said Hamish in his slow, sing-song voice. He put out a hand and laid it encouragingly on her arm. 'Let's think it through. What is the best thing for Bel? That's the first thing to consider.'

They both sat in silence for a few moments, looking out at the sheep milling around in the field in front of them.

Francie waited and, when he didn't speak, burst out, 'You said you thought it was right for Bel to live here. Don't you think so any longer?'

Hamish nodded slowly. 'Aye, I do think it's right. She belongs here.'

Francie smiled, realising how much she agreed with him.

He continued, 'It's right for her. But is it right for you? Maybe her parents are worried about imposing on you?'

'Oh.' Francie hadn't thought of that possibility. 'They never said anything about that.'

'But perhaps it is something you should discuss with them? If you're sure it is right for you. You've lived on your own for a number of years now, perhaps you prefer that.'

He watched her closely. Francie made herself think, not answer immediately. She thought of how it had been, living on her own at Tigh na Mara, having nobody to worry about but herself. She shook her head. 'No, I wouldn't prefer that. I know I have lots of friends here, good ones like you, but it can still get lonely living on your own.'

'Aye, it can,' said Hamish, not looking at her. After a moment he said, 'Well, that's one thing decided. You are happy to have Bel, and she is happy to live with you.'

'That's two things.'

'Yes, it is, isn't it?' He gave her a slow smile. 'Now we need to consider how we persuade her parents that this is a good idea.'

Francie had been cheered by his words so far, but now she felt depressed again. How could she explain to her son and his wife that their precious younger daughter would be better living away from them? They were going to be hurt and she hated the idea of hurting them.

'It's not going to be easy,' she said gloomily. 'I thought things were supposed to get easier as you got older?'

'Whatever gave you that idea?' said Hamish. 'Why don't we think it over for a couple of days and see what we come up with? Now I'd best get back to those last sheep, I don't like to keep them penned up too long.'

'Yes, of course. I'm sorry to disturb you.'

'It's always a pleasure to see you. And I definitely needed a break.' Hamish rose to his feet and stretched gingerly. 'Perhaps I'm getting too old for this, it never used to seem such hard work.'

'You mustn't do too much, you know,' said Francie, concerned. Hamish had always seemed the fittest, the least changing of all her old crofter friends. 'You've got to look after yourself.'

'I'll be fine.'

As Francie drove the meandering road back to Strathan, she decided to invite Hamish for a meal in a couple of days' time. In fact, it would be a big help to him if he didn't have to cook for himself so much, perhaps she should make a habit of inviting him over a few times a week. She would like that, and she hoped he would, too.

A Plan Forms

Lal was heading back to Tigh na Mara to be there for her parents' arrival. Her thoughts were still on arrangements at Anka's place, whether she'd secured the gate to the goats' pen and given the pig enough feed. She didn't notice Gran until she was at the car door, pulling it open. 'Is Bel with you? Have you seen her?'

'Er . . . no.' Lally was puzzled. 'I was expecting her to be here.'

'I popped over to see old Mrs Marsh and when I got back she'd gone. I was trying to persuade her to bake a cake for when your parents arrive, but she hasn't done that either.'

Lal felt a stirring of disquiet. Bel hadn't been keen to do anything much lately. She certainly hadn't wanted to see their parents, who were still intent on taking her home with them at the end of their visit. But for her to disappear was totally out of character, she was normally meticulous about telling adults of her plans.

'Have you tried her mobile?' she said, without much hope. Bel wasn't keen on her mobile and rarely switched it on. She said why bother, who would phone her? Unlike most teenagers, she didn't seem fond of texting.

'I tried, it's switched off.'

The two women stared at each other, Lal's own blank expression reflected on his grandmother's face. Where could Bel have gone?

'Maybe she just felt like a walk?' she said doubtfully.

'In this?' The wind was getting up, flattening the grass to the hillside.

'Let's have a cup of tea and think some more,' said Lal. Doing something was better than doing nothing. As they sat at the little kitchen table, nursing mugs in their hands, she said, 'How about trying Hamish? Bel is very fond of him, she might have cycled over there to have a chat. In fact, have you checked her bike? If that hasn't gone she can't be far away.'

'It has gone. And I've already phoned Hamish. He hasn't seen her, but says he'll keep an eye open.'

They sat in silence for a few minutes. Then Lal said, 'Harbour House! Maybe she's getting the Bothy ready. It was good of Iain to lend it to Mum and Dad, wasn't it?'

'The Bothy is already ready,' Gran said, but she checked the drawer where they kept Iain's spare key. 'The key's still here, I don't think she'll be down there.'

'I'll go and check, just in case.'

Lally threw on a waterproof against the rain that was starting and ran the short distance to the neighbouring house. She tried the Bothy, but it was empty. For good measure, she searched the ruins of the house and the barns. No sign of either Bel or her bike.

She turned and struggled back up the hill against the increasing wind.

'She's not there,' she said to Gran. She didn't think either of them had really thought she would be.

Lal looked out at the wild weather and shuddered. She knew Bel loved it when the elements threw all they had at the fragile earth, but surely even she wouldn't want to be out in this?

A knock at the door a few minutes later raised their hopes momentarily, but it was only Hamish.

'I came across as quickly as I could,' he said, shaking rain drops from his curly hair. 'No word, hmm? There was no sign of her on the road, or of anyone else for that matter. No-one wants to be out on a day like this.'

'She's taken her bike,' said Lal. 'But where can she have cycled to?'

They phoned the shop at Drummore, in the vain hope she had suddenly remembered they were short of some vital ingredient, but there had been no sign of her there.

'Mum and Dad will be here any minute,' said Lal. 'Thank goodness Ant decided not to come with them. But what are we going to say?'

'That they shouldn't have put pressure on Bel to go home with them.' Gran's face was unusually grim. 'That's what has put her up to this, I'm sure.'

'Poor wee lass,' said Hamish.

'Yes, I know. But where can she have gone? She can't just have disappeared.'

'Do you think we should maybe contact the police?' said Hamish, making Lal's heart sink more than ever. Gran said she was sure that wasn't necessary yet, but Lal knew it would be the first thing her parents insisted on once they arrived.

Which is exactly what they did do. They ran over all the possibilities Lal and her grandmother had already considered, Mum looking paler and Dad grimmer with every minute.

Then Lal's dad said, 'She's been missing for hours now, and the weather is getting worse. We have to phone the police.'

Lal and Gran looked at each other.

Surely it couldn't have come to that?

'She's hiding somewhere, I'm sure she is,' said Gran. 'We don't need to involve the police, do we? It's not as if she's been kidnapped.'

'How do you know she hasn't?' Mum's voice was faint.

Lal sat down beside her and squeezed her arm. 'I think Gran's right. We know Bel was upset about — things. She really didn't want to go back to Glasgow.'

'Even if she had intended to hide, how do we know she hasn't hurt herself?' Dad was pacing the room. 'Where could she hide in weather like this? It's not as if she has any friends in the area.'

There was silence for a while as they all considered his words. Lal's head was spinning. Where could Bel have gone? Where would she have gone?

It was Hamish who spoke first. He had been quiet since the arrival of Lal's parents, fading politely into the background. Now he said slowly, 'What about Morag Kirkpatrick? Didn't you

236

say the two lassies were getting a wee bit friendly?'

'I don't know . . . ' said Lal, thinking how Bel hadn't returned Morag's more recent phone calls, but Gran had already hurried to find the local phone directory and searched out the number. Any possibility was worth pursuing.

They stood around her as she made the call, hanging on to every word that Gran said and trying desperately to make out the other half of the conversation. It seemed to be Morag herself who answered, but she hadn't seen Bel and said she hadn't spoken to her for days. She expressed sympathy and concern and promised to ask her brother, Lachlan, if he had any news as soon as he came in.

Gran was just about to replace the phone when they all heard Morag's tone change. 'Hang on a minute, I can hear . . . goodness, Lachy you're soaked . . . I don't suppose you've seen anything of . . . Bel! Bel, you're here! What on earth has been happening?'

'Bel's there,' said Gran, sitting down suddenly on a kitchen chair. 'They've got her.'

'Let me talk,' said Lal's dad, taking the phone.

Lal was petrified in case he started shouting at Bel, but his voice was low and calm as he made sure the child was safe and then obtained directions to the house. Bel was all right. The worry was over. It was hard to take it all in.

'I'm coming with you,' said Lal as her parents got up to leave. 'Is she really OK?'

'So she says. We'll see for ourselves soon enough.' Dad gave a shiver and closed his eyes for a moment. He had held himself together, but now Lal saw how terrified he had been, which made her feel her own fear all over again.

'It's all fine now,' she said.

They hurried out to the still-unpacked car, leaving Hamish to potter around making tea and soothing Gran with his gentle chatter.

Lal and Bel and Gran and their parents were all sitting around the table after an excellent Sunday dinner. The meal had been a little subdued, as they had all been since the euphoria of Bel's return home the previous day.

It was brilliant that Bel was safe, but they still hadn't really addressed the reason why she had run off like that, scaring them all.

They had discovered the bare bones of what had happened. How Bel had intended to hide away in a beach-side shack she had visited with Morag and Lachlan. How the boy had found her there and instead of falling in with her plans, as she had expected, had insisted on taking her to his home. If he hadn't discovered her, who knew how long it would have been before she was discovered?

'I think it's perhaps time we all had a chat,' said her father, pushing away the bowl from which he had scraped every last trace of the apple crumble and cream. 'Now all of us are here together it seems like a good time.'

'A very good idea,' said Gran, although she looked a little flustered. 'Wait until I've made the coffee and then we can have a good long talk.'

Bel jumped up to help her and Lal and her parents busied themselves stacking the bowls and other debris and carrying it through to the kitchen. Lal wanted to ask what her parents had decided, but didn't dare.

'Right,' said her father when they had all settled down once again. 'First of all I want to say how grateful we are to your gran for having you two girls staying here for so long.'

'It's been a pleasure,' said Gran quickly. 'They were doing me a favour part of the time, as you know. And of course, Lal is now helping Anka.'

'Now we need to talk about the future,' continued Peter Dunmore, not raising his voice, but making it clear he wanted them all to listen. It made Lal realise what a good lecturer he must be, with that quiet authority. 'Sally and I had a chance to discuss things this morning.' He touched his wife's hand and she smiled at him tremulously. 'We agree that we haven't handled this situation with Bel, this bullying, nearly as well as we should have done.'

Bel looked uncomfortable at the blunt use of the word 'bullying' and even opened her mouth as though to speak, but her father continued. 'We didn't want to believe it could be as bad as it obviously was. We were wrong not to spot what was happening at the time and wrong not to be more sympathetic when we were told about it. When we get back to Glasgow we're going to take it up properly with the school, insist that they deal with these other girls.'

Bel opened her mouth again, looking horrified, but her father gestured for her to wait.

'This needs to be sorted out whether you go back to that school or not. If you were being bullied, no doubt others are too. The school has to deal with that. But the main concern for all of us here is Bel's own future.'

Lal could see her sister looking anxiously from one parent to the other, but this time she didn't try to speak.

'Your mother and I would love it, if you came back home with us. We've missed you during the months you've been away.'

'It's so quiet,' said his wife, smiling gently. 'We knew it would only be the two of us one day, but we didn't expect it so soon. We miss you, Bel.'

'However,' continued Peter, 'We have talked this over and realised the most important thing is to decide what is best for you. Your gran says she is happy for you to stay here, would in fact welcome it. Lal seems to think that this area suits you and that you're happy here. So, if you want to stay, you can stay.'

'I can?' Bel looked stunned for a moment, and then slowly her broad, metal-clad smile appeared. She jumped to her feet. 'Are you serious? Really?' She rushed to hug each of her parents in turn, and then Gran. 'I can stay here? I can't believe it!'

Her parents exchanged a small, rather sad smile. 'You mustn't think you are being rewarded for giving us that huge shock by running away yesterday. What you did was wrong. It was silly and dangerous. Thank goodness that young boy had the sense to make you go back to his house.'

'He said I was crazy and the shack roof leaked. Which it did.'

'You must promise me two things,' continued her father in the same grave voice. 'Never to keep your difficulties bottled up but to talk to us about them. In return, we promise to listen. And secondly, to work hard at your studies and to help your gran around the croft as much as she wishes. Moving out here is not going to be a soft option for you.'

'I promise,' said Bel, her eyes shining. She looked better than she had in weeks, bright and bubbly and full of hope. Lal was delighted with her parents' decision. It was the one she hoped they would make. But when she realised how hard it was for them, how much they were obviously going to miss Bel, she also felt sad. Why was life never simple?

'We'll have to look into this whole home-schooling thing and see how we set it up,' said her mother. 'We're going to get very computer-savvy ourselves and do all we can to help. If you're sure that is the way you want to go?'

'Actually,' said Bel, looking around at them all, 'Actually, I was wondering if I shouldn't give the school in Ullapool a try. Morag and Lachy say it's not that bad.'

Lal felt a grin spreading across her own face. This really was good news. 'You'd give it a go, even with all the travelling?'

'Morag says the bus isn't that bad, you can use the time to do some of your homework. Lachy says that is rubbish, but he says it's a laugh.'

Lal sat back as her parents and Bel discussed this new plan, Gran chipping in occasionally. The details of it didn't matter to Lally, it was the huge stride forward Bel had made. Friends. She really had made friends here, young people, and that was the very best thing for her. It was going to be all right.

Family Secrets

Iain was travelling the long road to Strathan for the third time in four months, and this time with his parents not so far behind him. He had, conscientiously, offered to drive them the last couple of hundred miles from Edinburgh, but they had declined and said they could find their way perfectly well themselves. Iain wasn't sure his father's Mercedes would find it easy to negotiate the narrow roads after Inverloch, but he decided not to say so.

As he drove the last, snake-like bends, he felt his spirits rise. Even more than on his second visit, he was drawn to this place, desperate to see around the last corner, to view the sandstone archway and the wide bay and then Harbour House itself. Yes, he was here. Now he could finally relax.

Which was ridiculous, because he

hardly knew the place. And he wasn't staying at Harbour House this time. He had accepted the invitation to stay at Tigh na Mara with the Dunmores, and he was sure to regret that. Despite his desire to see Lal again, he really didn't know the family that well. To stay with them in that tiny cottage with its basic facilities was bound to lead to problems.

He couldn't decide whether to go to Harbour House first, and see that everything was fine, or to call in at Tigh na Mara and announce his arrival. He was saved from having to make a decision by the appearance of young Bel climbing up the beach from Strathan Bay. She recognised his car and raised a hand.

She was already at his window as he drew to a halt. 'You're here! Great. We didn't know what time to expect you. Gran has everything ready and she's so looking forward to having a real visitor. Family don't count, you know. Do you want to come and drop off your bags?

Where are your parents? We're all dying to meet them.'

Iain wasn't sure whether to smile or sigh. Bel was always just a little bit more than he felt ready to deal with.

He glanced down over the sands of the bay and saw that once again there were surfers out, making the most of the waves.

'Were you watching the surfers?' he said. 'I thought you didn't approve of them using the bay here?'

'Approve?' The girl looked puzzled. 'Why wouldn't I approve? Surfing is an excellent sport, people don't realise how much you can do here. Lachy's going to give me some lessons as soon as we can get my wetsuit out of the attic.'

'Good for you,' said Iain pleased and surprised at this change in the youngster. 'Now, are you going to get in and come up to Tigh na Mara with me, or shall I go on my own?'

She grinned her wide smile. 'You're coming straight to us? Oh goodie. Yes, I'd love a lift. I pretend to Gran and Lal that I don't mind slogging up and down that hill, but actually it'll be nice to be driven for a change.' She climbed in. 'And did you know I'm going to be living at Strathan from now on? I'm going to go to school in Ullapool, I've chosen all my subjects . . . '

So that was why the child was so happy. Iain smiled and was content to let her chatter on.

★ ★ ★

Iain Cunningham's parents were exactly as Lal had pictured them. Well-to-do, confident and ever so slightly disapproving.

Lal didn't know what they had to be disapproving of. Strathan was looking its late-summer best, although there were clouds in the west that suggested this might not last too much longer.

She hadn't been there when Iain welcomed them to the Bothy and showed them around Harbour House, but apparently they weren't too impressed.

'My mother's worried about the steps up to the bed platform, perhaps I should just have found them a bed and breakfast,' said Iain.

'Once they try it out they're bound to see how wonderful it is. And they do know they're eating here tonight, so they don't have to worry about cooking?'

'Yes, I explained your gran had invited them. They said they'd planned to try one of the local hotels, but I think the last bit of the drive here showed them that there aren't any very local hotels . . . ' He shook his head wryly and Lal grinned to herself. A few months ago Iain himself would have been expecting to find any number of high class establishments on his door-step.

Gran and Bel set up a table in the conservatory in honour of their guests and recognition that really the kitchen wasn't big enough for more than four people. Although the nights were just beginning to draw in, it being the end of August, it was still light outside and they had a magnificent view of the clouds massing over the northern mountains.

'There's going to be a big storm, brilliant,' said Bel, peering out. 'I hope there's thunder and lightning and everything, I love that.'

'It certainly looks like it will be a wild and windy one,' said Gran happily.

Iain's mother's expression changed from mildly concerned to anxious. 'You're very exposed up here. Will everything be all right? And that house of Iain's hasn't even got a roof.'

'It's stood for years, it'll be fine for a while longer,' said Iain, and then added in an aside to Lal, 'Although I really should get the roof put on before winter. Did I tell you I've contacted the McMichaels and they're coming round to look tomorrow?'

Lal smiled her approval whilst trying to keep track of the main conversation between Gran and his parents. Gran was up to something, she was sure. She wished she knew what it was.

Even Iain's parents, John and Vivien, had to thaw eventually under Gran's determined friendliness. She had also produced a delicious meal, local smoked salmon followed by a joint of venison roasted as only Gran knew how.

She presented the whole meal in a slightly more formal way than usual, with baby new potatoes from the garden and three different vegetables.

It was impressive, and in case the visitors didn't notice Bel took the trouble to point this out to them, emphasising the local provenance of so much good food, not to mention the skill with which it was all cooked.

'And Bel is no mean cook herself,' said Iain, also relaxing as the meal went on. 'She makes the best scones ever.'

'I wish I had more time for home-baking,' said his mother. Lal noted her immaculate hands and perfect outfit and didn't think she was the sort of person who would indulge in much home-baking, even if she did have 'time'. Come to think of it, as the woman didn't appear to work, what on earth did she occupy herself with?

'And what do you think of Harbour House?' Gran asked finally, as she brought in a tray of coffee and chocolates.

'There's not much to see of the house, is there?' said Iain's father.

'The little place we're staying is very nice, of course,' said his wife. 'But I can't help wondering why John's Uncle Alexander didn't concentrate on fixing up the house.'

'He was going to do that next,' said Gran, looking sad. 'He had great plans for it.'

'And had ordered all the supplies,' said Iain. 'He was very organised. And obviously very good at what he did. The work on the Bothy is top class.'

'Yes, he was good at everything he did,' agreed Gran. 'He was all together a lovely man. It's a shame you didn't know him better.'

There was an awkward silence which Gran allowed to drag on. When no-one spoke she continued, 'He was very sad, you know, about the rift in the family.'

'He only had to make an effort to get in touch, if that's how he felt,' said Iain's father stiffly. Lal could almost feel him wanting to say, *and what has it got to do with you?*

Gran continued in her cheerful way, 'Sometimes it's difficult to be the one who makes the first move.'

'What was it that caused the rift?' asked Bel, looking eagerly from face to face. 'Do we know?'

John Cunningham cleared his throat. 'I've been looking into things a little since I talked to Iain about this. It has always seemed odd that my grandfather left everything to my father.'

Gran said, 'Sandy was quite clear that his parents had the right to leave their business to whoever they chose.' Lal smiled faintly to herself.

Gran obviously knew far more about Sandy's past than she had divulged so far. She was definitely up to something. Lal could tell.

'And John's father was the one who

worked in the business,' said his wife defensively. 'He worked very hard, built it up to a new level.'

John nodded. 'He was very proud of the firm, what he'd achieved with it. I think it wasn't in a very good state when he took over, but he managed not only to pull it through, but to expand. Hopefully my older son and I are continuing on that path. Of course, Iain would have been very welcome to join us, I certainly don't think it should be a choice of one son or the other.'

'That's very kind,' said Iain awkwardly. 'And fine if both sons were interested . . . '

'If you're not interested, we're happy with that too,' said his father.

'You are?' Iain stared at him, looking quite stunned. 'But I always thought you were disappointed.'

'We've never been disappointed in you,' said his father, and his mother nodded and smiled.

Lal watched Iain and was delighted when, after a moment, he gave a tentative smile in return.

'Do you think your grandfather thought it had to be one son or the other?' asked Gran keen to stick to the point. 'And that's what caused the division? I think Sandy had hoped for some support from the family in his chosen career at sea and was hurt that he didn't get it. Not that it did him any harm. He did well in the end, rose to be ship's captain.'

John took a sip of his good, strong coffee and cleared his throat once more. 'I don't think it's true to say my Uncle Alexander had no help from the family. I've been wracking my brains to see if I can remember anything about why he left, and I recalled there was something about money. I've looked through some letters of my father's and it appears a significant amount of money went, er, missing at that time. My grandfather chose not to prosecute his own son, but I don't think he ever forgave him for it.'

'You're saying that Sandy was a thief?' gasped Lal. 'I don't believe it!'

'I'm not saying anything, just reporting what I found. It seems from the letter that so much money was taken the factory almost had to close. That's not something you can make up.'

'What makes you think it was Sandy?'

'His father certainly believed it was.'

'But Sandy . . . ' said Lal, looking at Gran for support. 'He would never do something like that.'

'I agree with Lal,' said Gran, but calmly, not at all as though this revelation was a surprise. 'I don't think Sandy took the money either. But clearly something happened. What a shame this mystery was left to destroy the family. That no-one tried to discover the truth.'

'My grandfather and father thought they already knew the truth,' said John stiffly. 'As far as they were concerned, that was the end of the matter.'

'But if he didn't steal the money,' said Bel, leaning forward eagerly. 'Then who did? We need to know!'

'It's far too long ago to find out the details now,' said John. 'I certainly haven't time to do any more searching.'

'But perhaps I could,' said Iain, looking slowly from his parents to Lal's gran and back. 'I'm pretty good at trawling through old records, either on-line or on paper. I could come down for a few days, see what I can find. I think I'd like to know the truth, if it was possible.'

'Good for you,' said Gran. 'I know Sandy pretended that this was all in the past and it didn't worry him, but he talked about it a lot towards the end. I feel he would like it to be resolved, for people to know what happened.'

'Maybe that's why he left you Harbour House,' said Bel excitedly, clutching Iain's arm. 'Maybe he knew you'd be the one to solve the mystery for him!'

'Bel, this isn't some kind of adventure story,' said Lal.

'But it feels like one. I think it's brilliant!'

'Having a thief in the family came as something of a shock to me,' said Iain's father, with markedly less enthusiasm.

'We don't know for sure Sandy was a thief,' protested Bel, who clearly thought she knew he definitely was not.

'If this means that Iain comes to spend a little time at home, then I for one won't be sorry,' said Vivien, smiling for almost the first time. 'It would be good to see you back. And I'm sure your brother would be keen to help.'

Lal finally warmed to the older woman. She did love her son, for all her apparent coolness. She wanted him to spend time with his family. That was the way things should be.

'This has been a very interesting discussion,' said Gran, smiling now. Lal suspected she had got exactly what she wanted. 'I'm so glad we've managed to have it. Now can I get anybody more coffee, or perhaps a wee dram of whisky?'

The older Cunninghams took this as their cue for departure and after assuring Gran they could manage breakfast for themselves, and agreeing they would see Iain in the morning, they headed out into the darkening night.

★   ★   ★

Iain thought he was never going to get any time alone with Lally. He was pleased his parents had deigned to visit Harbour House, and seemed to be enjoying their holiday, but he was surprised how much time they expected to spend with him. They weren't generally a family who did a lot together.

His father even accompanied him when he showed the McMichaels the work that needed doing on Harbour House. To Iain's surprise, he seemed to think re-roofing the place was the right thing to do. 'It doesn't mean you can't sell it later, if that's what you decide.'

It was quite a relief when, on the last day, they expressed a wish to drive up to Cape Wrath and see the lighthouse there. Iain excused himself, saying he needed to catch up on work e-mails, but secretly vowing to track Lally down.

She had been very busy on the croft belonging to the Norwegian woman, but had agreed to take some time off. He was determined to make the most of it.

He suggested they walk out to the headland and she seemed happy with the idea. They kitted themselves out in sensible walking boots (Iain had invested in a pair since his first visit to Harbour House) and waterproofs, just in case, and set off.

It was a blustery day with clouds scudding across the sky. They followed the grassy pathway that skirted the top of the bay, past Harbour House itself, and out towards the wilder parts of the promontory.

It was only when they were out of sight of Tigh na Mara that Iain felt they were safe from being joined by Bel, or called back by Lal's gran, and he could relax.

He wished he felt confident enough to take Lally's hand, but he didn't. Instead he said, 'How is the croft work going? It's certainly keeping you busy.'

She shot him one of her bright smiles. 'It's fun, I'm enjoying it. Although there is an awful lot to do.'

'Is it something you might consider, trying to get your own croft?'

'Oh, no, I don't think so. This is just temporary.'

'But maybe better than no job at all?' suggested Iain, before he could stop himself. It was hard to picture being Lally, not knowing what she was going to do with her future. Perhaps it was because she was so young. He didn't think he had ever been that young.

Lal grinned at him, pulling the scrunchy from her wild hair and trying, not very successfully, to tie it into a more secure ponytail. 'I do need to think about getting a proper job, don't I?' She pulled a face. 'I just wish I knew what that proper job was, and where it should be.'

'Maybe something will turn up,' said Iain and their eyes met and they both laughed at exactly the same time. He had never felt so in tune with anyone.

He took her hand, as though to help her across a burn, and held on to it once they were on the other side.

They walked out to the place where you could stand over the stone archway and look down to see absolutely nothing below you but the pounding sea. The wind was even wilder here and after a couple of moments they moved on around the headland to where it was more sheltered.

'Are you happy to go further?' asked Lally, to his delight. Initially he hadn't been sure if she had accepted his invitation merely out of politeness.

'Definitely.'

'If we go to the next headland you can see round to our own little lighthouse at Sturr. It's quite a nice walk. Perhaps your parents could have walked round to see that and not needed to make the long drive to Cape Wrath.'

'They're not very keen on walking,' said Iain quickly. 'And, actually, it's quite good to have a day without them.'

'They seem very nice,' said Lal at once. 'Do you think they're enjoying their visit?'

'Yes, I think they are. And yes, they are all right, really.' Iain felt as though he was making a huge admission as he said this. 'I don't usually spend much time with them, as you've probably gathered. I always felt they disapproved of the fact that I didn't want to go into the family business.'

'Just like Sandy.'

'Maybe not just like Sandy,' said Iain, remembering the accusations of theft that he had promised to look in to. 'But I suppose I can see how something like that could lead to discord.'

'I'm glad things are better between you and your parents.'

'Yes.' Iain didn't want to talk about that now so he turned the subject to one he was far more interested in — Lally.

The rest of the walk passed off brilliantly, the two of them chatting away as though they had known each other for years. Iain didn't want it to end, and Lally seemed to be enjoying herself too, but eventually they turned and headed for home. He was sorry he had to leave the following day.

The Past Returns

Francie worked methodically through her morning chores, and thought how strange it was to be here on her own. Bel was off for her first day at the local high school, and if she had been a little quiet as they waited for the bus, she hadn't had that tense, fixed look on her face that mention of school in Glasgow always brought.

Lal was busy at Achmore. She had been rather thoughtful since Iain's departure. Francie hoped something was developing between her older granddaughter and that nice young man. Time would tell.

She finished her first round of duties by about eleven, and rewarded herself with a mug of milky coffee and a rest in the conservatory. This was where Hamish found her.

'Come in, come in,' she said,

surprised and pleased to see him. 'Coffee? Or would you prefer tea?'

It was only when they were both settled in the cane chairs that she realised he didn't seem his normal calm self.

'Is Suzie all right?' she asked, alarmed.

He smiled. 'Suzie's fine. I left her in the garden with Pup. They're getting to be good friends.' He hesitated and then said, 'Bel get off to school all right?'

'Yes, fine. I took her to catch the bus at the village hall. Morag and Lachlan get on at Clashnessie. She'll be fine.'

'Of course she will.'

They sat in silence for a while and Francie began to grow uncomfortable. Normally silences with Hamish were not a problem, but she sensed that today was different.

'I was at the doctor's again yesterday,' he said finally, turning his mug in his hands.

'Oh.' Now Francie knew there was something wrong. Hamish always seemed so healthy, but since admitting the shearing had been a wee bit too much for him he had agreed to see a doctor. 'What did he say?' she said, trying to be brave. Surely nothing could be seriously wrong with him? She had lost her dear Billy, and then her good friend, Sandy. She didn't know how she would cope with losing Hamish.

'Nothing serious, I'm glad to say.'

'That's good.' Francie gave a long sigh of relief. She put down her mug. Her hands were trembling too much to hold it properly.

'A wee bit of angina, Dr Morris said. It's fine how they can do all these tests in the surgery now and then send them away to the big hospital. He's given me some tablets to try, and says I should take things a little easier on the croft. But generally he said not to worry.'

'I'm so glad,' said Francie, smiling broadly now. What was a bit of angina at their age? She had one or two aches and pains herself, and Lal was always telling her to slow down, but you just had to do the best you could.

'Having this happen has given me a

wee bit of a shock,' said Hamish. 'I suppose I've always thought things would go on as they were. This has made me realise that I'm getting older.'

'We're all getting older.'

'Aye. And I've come to see that if there are things I want to do, I should do them now.'

'Ah,' said Francie, as though she understood, but she didn't. 'And there are things you want to do?'

'One or two, aye.' He smiled at her properly for the first time, seeming to get into his stride. 'I'd like to tell you about them?'

'Of course.'

'First of all, I've a mind to give up the croft.'

This was the very last thing Francie could have expected. This was the croft his family had run for over a hundred years. He had even been born in that house. She was horrified. 'But this has been in the McDougall family for generations.'

'One or two. But it's just a place,

Francie. And it's a lot of work for one person. It made me realise, when I cleared out all the old machinery, that I've just been scraping the surface for a while now. Keeping things ticking over. I'm slowing down and maybe what the place needs is a younger pair of hands. You know there's a waiting list for crofts around here, so if I give up the lease there's a good chance we'll get some youngsters moving in.'

'I see you've thought this through.'

'I've done a lot of thinking over the last couple of weeks.'

'So you're going away?' Francie could feel a lump starting to grown in her throat. She had thought Hamish would be here for ever, as solid and reliable as the land itself.

'I thought I might do a wee bit of travelling, before I'm really too old. I've a yen to visit that cousin of mine who moved to Canada.'

'You're moving to Canada?'

'No, no, I just thought I'd go for a wee visit. He's always asking me to.'

'It's a long way, for someone who hasn't travelled much,' said Francie cautiously. She didn't mean to be discouraging, but the thought of Hamish, in his darned jerseys and wellington boots, navigating his way through international airports — well, it was hard to take in.

'Aye, it is. But you've often said that if people put their minds to something, they can do it.'

'Ye-es,' said Francie doubtfully. The sorts of things she'd envisaged people putting their minds to were repainting the village hall, not travelling to the other end of the world.

'And, the thing is, I wouldn't want to do it on my own.' Now Hamish's initial unease seemed to return. He glanced at Francie, and then down at his work-roughened hands. 'I was wondering, it's probably a ridiculous idea, but I wondered whether you would consider . . . '

'Yes?' said Francie, feeling rather breathless.

'I wondered if you and I could . . . no, I know it's a ridiculous idea.

But I thought now was the time to be decisive, to go for what I wanted. Of course I see now I was wrong.'

'Hamish, I can't answer you unless you actually ask me a question.'

'Yes, of course, yes.' He took a deep breath, his round face suffused with colour. 'Francie, I don't suppose you'd consider marrying again?'

For a moment she was speechless. She had hoped he was inviting her to travel with him. But this! It took her breath away for a moment. And then she realised it was exactly what she wanted to do. Until he began this strange conversation, this thought would never have occurred to her. Now she answered with conviction, 'If I was marrying you, I would.'

Hamish's anxious expression turned into a shy smile. 'Really?' he said softly, as though he couldn't believe it.

'Yes, really,' said Francie, taking his hand and feeling herself blush, which she didn't think she had done for years. She felt excited. Hamish was right.

There was so much they could still do, and how lovely to do it together.

* * *

Iain began his research into the money that had gone missing from his great-grandfather's business. Somehow he felt he couldn't make decisions about anything else until this was sorted out. He didn't specify to himself what he meant by 'anything else', but it definitely had something to do with Lally Dunmore.

He started his search by going online and finding out as much about the company as he could. He had always believed that Cunningham Carpets Limited was a family business begun by his great-grandfather. He was surprised, however, to discover that a small business had existed in the family even before his great-grandfather's time. He also found that the business didn't become a limited company until the late 1940s, which would be around the time Great Uncle Alex had left home.

This meant that before that time the business had not been required to file accounts so there was nothing Iain could find relating to that. He did do a trawl of the local newspapers to see if there was any story relevant to his search, but that came up blank too.

The next step was a visit home, which he arranged for a weekend in September.

It felt odd returning to Buckinghamshire and actually being pleased to do so. He knew his parents were looking forward to his visit and realised it would be rather nice to see Stephen and his family again. Now it was accepted that he, Iain, would never join the family firm, everything seemed so much easier. He was still part of the family. That was the main thing.

His father no longer seemed to resent the fact that Harbour House had been left to Iain. They had all decided that that was Great Uncle Alexander's decision and it wasn't for them to question it. What was left for them to do was find out what had happened around the time

Great Uncle Alex had himself left home.

He arrived at his parents' house late on the Friday evening and began his research first thing on Saturday morning. The factory was empty. His father came with him to open up the offices, but then went off for his usual Saturday morning round of golf. Iain was pleased when his brother, Stephen arrived shortly afterwards.

'I know I'm not a whizz with records like you are,' he said. 'But I thought I might be able to lend a hand. At least I know where all the old files are kept, because I'm the one who moved them last.'

He led the way to the basement of the office block and when Iain saw the boxes and boxes of files, he was even more relieved to have his brother's help. This was going to take longer than he had anticipated.

'I thought Dad might have stuck around, to keep an eye on me if nothing else,' he said, frowning around the dusty room.

'I think Dad's a bit afraid of what we might find.'

'Afraid?'

'Yes, after all, if family money was taken and if it wasn't Great Uncle Alex, the obvious next suspect is our own grandfather. He would have had access to the money, along with our great-grandfather. I'm sure Dad's thought of that himself. It's not a nice thought, is it, that your dad might be a thief?'

'No. Nor your great uncle,' said Iain, surprised to find himself wanting to clear Sandy's name. 'Anyway, let's get started. Making wild guesses isn't going to help us.'

Instead of objecting to Iain's tone, and wanting to take the lead himself, as he would once have done, Stephen merely shrugged and agreed.

'I think there's maybe something here. Maybe.' Iain sat back on his heels and wiped his face with a dusty hand. If was Sunday afternoon and he was seriously regretting his claim to be good at sorting through old documents.

276

The whole of Saturday had turned up nothing. This morning Stephen had decided he should spend time with his wife and toddler son, but had returned after lunch.

He too sat back from the folder he was paging through. 'What? I've even forgotten what we're looking for. And I can't believe anyone would keep so many useless pieces of paper.'

Iain tended to agree, but that discussion was for another day. 'Have you come across the name, Mary Cinderley, in the papers you've been going through?'

'Mary who? No, I don't think so. Or, hold on a minute, wasn't she a secretary or a clerk or something just after the war? I'm sure there was a Mary.'

'Yes, that's her. She seems to have been secretary to the Managing Director, who would have been our great-grandfather at that time.'

'What's so interesting about her?'

'I'm not sure.' Iain rubbed his forehead, probably leaving a dirty streak across it. 'There's just something . . . She seems to have been quite important, for a secretary. She signed quite a lot of letters herself, you can see it from these carbon copies. And then, suddenly, she's gone. She seems to have left around the same time Great Uncle Alex did.'

The two brothers looked at each other, eyes narrowed, trying to make sense of it. Could it be significant? Iain found he just wasn't sure. It felt odd, somehow, but his brain was bleary with being shut in a stuffy office for two days.

'Do you think she ran off with Great Uncle Alex?' said Stephen doubtfully.

'I don't know. I just think there's something odd about her. Let's finish here for now. Later I'll do some research on the genealogy websites, see if I can find out who she was, where she went.'

'Excellent idea,' said Stephen, sounding relieved. 'I know Mum's expecting us all for some kind of fancy high tea. I'll phone Lizzie and tell her we're finished here. I can collect her and the baby on our way.'

Iain smiled to himself as he followed

his brother out to their cars. Unexpectedly, he was enjoying seeing more of his brother, but it still felt strange to be participating in this happy family life.

He had previously wondered why Stephen spent so much time with their parents, suspected him of currying favour with them. Now it seemed that it was because he wanted to do it. Iain could even see why. Once he stopped being so defensive, he enjoyed spending time with his parents too.

It was later in the evening that Iain was finally able to escape from the family gathering (even in his more mellow state, there was only so much socialising he could cope with) and set up the laptop in his bedroom.

He logged on to a couple of the websites that specialised in births, marriages and deaths and put in what little he knew about Mary Cinderley.

He and Stephen had asked their father if he remembered her, but he had pointed out he hadn't even been born when she worked for the company and so had been no help.

Whilst he was waiting for the various searches to finish, Iain checked his e-mails. His heart did a strange little skip when he saw one was from Lally Dunmore.

The e-mail didn't say much. Just reiterated how much Gran had enjoyed having him to stay and telling a little about Bel's first weeks at school. Apparently, now the child had decided to go to the school, she was embracing the whole experience with enthusiasm.

Lal also mentioned her work for Anka was coming to an end.

This gave Iain the opportunity he had been looking for. He took a deep breath and began to type.

I'd really like to see you again soon. I don't think I can get up to Strathan for a few weeks, but if you're free why don't you come down to Edinburgh? I could find you a hotel if your friend hasn't room for you to stay. I miss you.

There. For the first time he had put his cards on the table, made his interest unmistakably clear. He pressed 'send' quickly before he could have second thoughts.

After that, it took a few moments to clear his head sufficiently to return to his search for Mary. He didn't find any concrete leads, but made a note of a couple of possibilities and decided to call it a day.

He had meetings in London in the morning and then the long journey back to Edinburgh. He hoped that by the time he got there he would have a visit from Lally to look forward to.

★　★　★

It was a couple of evenings later that Iain finally managed to return to his search for Mary Cinderley. He had begun by trying to link her to Great Uncle Alexander, as Stephen had suggested.

He remembered Lal said Sandy had

once been married. However, after a fair amount of searching it became clear that this marriage had happened much later, to a girl from Portsmouth, and hadn't lasted long. No apparent connection to Mary there.

He decided to start looking further back, to see where this woman who had been so important in Cunningham Carpets had come from. It took a while, with a fair amount of crosschecking, but eventually he found a record of her birth.

That was when things began to get interesting. Mary Cinderley had been the illegitimate child of Margaret Cinderley Sanderson. Unusually for an illegitimate birth, the father was named on the birth certificate: it was a John William Cunningham.

Iain sat back and let out a long breath. He had been right. There was a connection. His great grandfather had been John William Cunningham. It was too much to believe that Mary coming to work in the family business had been purely a coincidence. Iain was sure she had come because it belonged to her father.

But this led to still more questions. Did John William Cunningham know who she was? Had anyone in the family known? And what had happened to make her leave suddenly soon after the war?

He picked up his phone and, after a moment's hesitation, dialled Stephen's number rather than his parents'. He suspected they would find this new information upsetting. Illegitimate children, even in the distant past, wouldn't fit with their view of the family. Best if he talked it over with Stephen first.

'So Mary was related to us?' said Stephen, once Iain had explained his discovery. 'Goodness. What was she? Our great aunt?'

'Great half-aunt, I suppose.'

'Do you think she's still alive?'

'I doubt it. She was quite a bit older than Grandad and Great Uncle Alex. Hold on, I think I've got her . . . Yes, it must be her. She died in Spain in 1980. She doesn't seem to have married. At that time she was called Mary Cinderley Cunningham Sanderson.'

'Cunningham. So she wanted the family name, even if she didn't want contact with us.'

'It seems so.'

'It's amazing what you can do with the Internet. I don't think I ever realised the potential it has. Or maybe that's just because you are so good at working it.'

'I'm nothing special,' said Iain modestly. 'And it is an amazing resource. You can do anything almost anywhere, these days.'

'So what happens now? What should we do about Mary?'

'I don't know. We've discovered some useful information, but I'm not sure we will ever know everything. There are some things even the Internet can't turn up, like the reasons why people did things.'

'But what do you think happened? You've got a theory, I can tell.'

'I've got a few theories, but how about this one?' Iain paused to work it out in his head. 'She broke the news to her father, our Great Grandfather, about who she was. Instead of welcoming into the family with open arms he sent her away, with a significant amount of money to make sure she kept her mouth shut.'

'That's horrible,' said Stephen. 'To think he would disown her. But I suppose it's plausible.'

'Or it may be she stole the money, because he refused to acknowledge her. You can imagine she might be bitter, if the two legitimate boys were going to inherit everything and she was to get nothing. We can only guess.'

'And how does this connect to Great Uncle Alex?'

'I'm not sure, but I think it does.'

'I suppose we'll need to tell Dad. He might know something, but I doubt it.'

'Let's not say anything yet. I'll go back and have another look through the files at the office. Now I know I am looking for something connected to

Mary maybe I'll turn up something new. And well done for tracking her down. Have you ever thought of becoming a detective?'

Iain laughed and declaimed any special talent. Nevertheless, it felt good to be praised by his brother.

'I'm Not Ambitious
Like You'

Lally was feeling thoroughly confused. She had been looking forward to this trip to Edinburgh and to seeing Iain again. And now, with the news of Gran and Hamish getting married, it had chased all other thoughts from her mind.

She was pleased for them, of course, but it was so unexpected. She had somehow thought Gran would be always be at Tigh na Mara, however unrealistic she knew that to be, and that things would stay the same there. Now there were plans for Gran and Hamish to marry — very soon, apparently — and then leave for a honeymoon in Canada.

Gran had been very hesitant about this part of the arrangement. She had only just agreed to Bel moving to Strathan and didn't think she should take off across the world. And Hamish was having second thoughts about leaving his darling Suzie behind.

Unless Lal really was planning to stay in Sutherland . . .

Lal still wasn't sure what she was planning, and was delighted with this part of the new arrangement. She would definitely stay at Tigh na Mara until the newlyweds returned home. Then, with Hamish giving up his own place, she doubted there would be room for her, and she would have to move on. She really hoped that by then she would have found out what it was she wanted to move on to.

Lal was staying with her friend, Rosie, but Iain had invited her to his flat for a meal on the evening of her arrival. He said she had cooked for him often and it was his turn to reciprocate. Lal was interested to see what he produced. She didn't anticipate that Iain had very great skills in this area, but she was willing to be proved wrong.

His flat, at least, was exactly as she

would have expected. In a new block near the waterfront in Leith, it was smart and convenient, but characterless.

Iain must have sensed her opinion as he saw her glance around on entering. 'I know it's a bit bland, but it suits me for the time being. It's only rented, so I'm not obliged to stay here long term.'

'It's very nice,' she said, accepting his kiss on the cheek and trying not to feel that it meant anything.

She handed him the bottle of wine she had brought and they exchanged news of their families as he poured them each a drink.

'It's great the new school is working out for Bel,' he said.

'It's brilliant. She's much happier, back to how she used to be a year or two ago. Seeing that has made me realise how she had gradually changed.' Lal shook her head. She still blamed herself for not having done something sooner.

'It's good she's happy now.'

Iain went to check whatever it was he

was cooking in the kitchen, and Lal remembered he hadn't heard the latest news, about Gran and Hamish.

She told him this when he returned, trying to keep her tone neutral.

'That's lovely,' he said, but the way he looked at her, his dark eyes so sympathetic, she felt her knew her feelings were mixed.

'Yes, it is, isn't it?' she said brightly. 'I think we were all a bit shocked. We all like Hamish, of course, but he's always seemed so stuck in his ways, a permanent bachelor. But if it's going to make Gran happy, which I really think it is, although I didn't realise she was unhappy . . . '

'It didn't strike me she was unhappy, but that doesn't mean to say this isn't an exciting development. Will the wedding be soon?'

'At the end of October.'

'So you'll stay on at Tigh na Mara whilst they're away?'

'Yes, I promised I would.'

'But what will you do for work?' he

asked, sounding annoyingly like her father.

'I'll look after the croft for Gran, and do her holiday cottages changeovers, although with summer coming to an end there won't be so many of those.' She paused before adding, 'And I can do more with the Historical Society. Things have rather lapsed while everyone has been so busy. Actually, I'm planning to visit the National Museum whilst I'm here, there's talk of them arranging a dig in the area where the axe head was found.' She hadn't mentioned this to anyone else and wasn't sure why she was telling Iain. 'I was wondering if I might have the chance to work on it.'

'That would be, er, different,' he said cautiously.

'It would be fun. But unfortunately it won't be until next year.' She sighed. 'I probably won't even be living in Strathan by then.'

'Are you still keen on setting up a museum and putting local finds on display?'

Lal remembered how he had originally poured scorn on her idea of a local museum and said defensively, 'Yes, and there are some very interesting ones!'

'I didn't say there weren't . . . '

'But you still think the idea is ridiculous.' Lal was hurt by his attitude and couldn't help letting her anger show.

Instead of apologising, Iain frowned. 'I still can't believe you passed up the chance of that job at the university. It made such good sense.'

'No, it didn't. It's not what I want. I'm not ambitious like you, I don't want a career in the conventional way.'

'But you're so able, Lal. Why waste your talents stuck away at Strathan?'

'I'm not wasting them,' snapped Lal. She had thought he was beginning to understand how she felt about Strathan, but clearly not. She was just about to tell him exactly what she thought of his opinions when something caught her attention.

'Iain, is that burning I can smell?'

It definitely was. They both leapt up and dashed to the kitchen.

'I was doing a roast,' said Iain, pulling open the oven door and allowing a wave of smoke to erupt out. 'My mother said you needed to get the oil very hot before you put the potatoes in. And then we started talking, and I forgot all about it . . .'

Lal had found a pair of new-looking oven gloves and used these to remove the smoking tray of oil from the oven. 'I don't think there's any harm done,' she said, as she carefully put it down. 'Although I suggest you don't use this oil to cook the potatoes in. Ugh, it smells awful.'

Iain turned up the extractor fan and opened a window. He looked sheepish. 'I'm so sorry. I wanted everything to be perfect. The meat is probably burnt too. I was doing so well at following the instructions until I got distracted talking to you.'

Lal smiled at seeing the calm and

collected Iain so disconcerted. For the moment, at least, their argument was forgotten. She concentrated on lowering the heat in the oven, turning the meat, and generally making sure the meal was going to be more or less edible.

'The idea was that you wouldn't have to do all the work, for once,' said Iain regretfully.

'I'm sorry, I'm taking over, aren't I? Do you want . . . ?'

'No, go ahead.' He looked relieved as well as embarrassed. 'Next time I'll take you out for a meal, I promise.'

The evening passed off fairly well, but Lal felt a constraint between them that wouldn't quite go away. They had a meal together a couple of evenings later, but that was no better. She couldn't help feeling Iain wanted her to be something she wasn't and never could be.

She returned to Strathan feeling disheartened.

★ ★ ★

Iain couldn't believe how stupid he had been. He was so desperate for Lal to move back to Edinburgh so he could see more of her. Now he had upset her, which was the last thing he wanted.

Of course, it would have been ideal if she could have been persuaded to see sense, but if she wouldn't it didn't mean they had to lose the relationship that was developing between them.

He hadn't even got round to telling Lal his and Stephen's suspicions about Mary Cinderley. He knew she would be pleased that Sandy no longer appeared to be the thief — if there had even been a thief — but things had been so stiff between them he hadn't found the right time to tell her.

He was still brooding on this when Stephen phoned to tell him he had done some more searching through the old records. 'And guess what I found?'

'I've no idea, but I hope you're going to tell me.'

'A large amount of money was taken out of the business around the time

Mary and Great Uncle Alex both left.'

'We know that already.'

'No, we know Dad believed that had happened. Now I've found proof that it did. There is even correspondence between our great grandfather and the bank saying only family had authority to draw that much cash. And the bank said it was signed for by a Cunningham and collected by the Managing Director's secretary as usual.'

'So it was Mary.'

'She collected the money, but she couldn't have signed the cheque. I've gone through the records and there were only three signatories: our great grandfather, our grandfather, and Great Uncle Alex.'

'So one of them must have signed it.' Iain scratched his head. 'Unless it was forged?'

'We'll never know for sure, but do you want to know what I think? I think Great Uncle Alex signed it, and that he gave the money to Mary. He must have found out who she was and decided she had a right to the money. That would have given her the funds to go and live in Spain. He'd already decided to leave the business himself. So they both departed, and the disappearance of the money is all hushed up. Families, eh? You never know what has been going on in them.'

'And despite all that, Great Uncle Alex still left Harbour House to me. Family was still important to him.'

'Yes. Maybe he thought you were being left out, as he seems to have felt he and Mary were. He was trying to make it up to you.'

'Well, he's certainly achieved one thing. It's brought us all closer together.'

'It has, hasn't it? Now we just need to break all this to Dad. He'll be interested, if a bit upset.'

'I'll leave that to you,' said Iain, glad he had the excuse of being too far away.

After that conversation Iain sat in his quiet, empty flat and pondered all they had learnt.

Lal would be pleased. It seemed certain her beloved Sandy wasn't a thief. He was a man trying to do the right thing. Even on his death, he had tried to do the right thing, to make sure things were shared fairly among the family.

Or maybe it was more than that. Maybe he had wanted a Cunningham to love Harbour House as he had done, to have the chance to live there.

He had given Iain that chance, as he had given Mary the chance to follow what had presumably been her dream.

Now Iain needed to decide what to do about it. He just didn't see how he could sort out his life. Edinburgh no longer felt right to him, but this was where he had to be for work.

Or did he?

Hadn't he said to Stephen he could do his kind of work almost anywhere?

His heart began to beat faster as he thought through the ramifications of that idea.

*　★　*

The nights were drawing in now and Strathan was taking on a whole new persona. This morning had seen the first frosts edging the frail blades of grass and the sky overhead was so pale it was almost white, as though it too was frozen. The sea lay still and grey with scarcely a ripple.

Lal hurried through her outdoor chores. She had plans for a mammoth bout of baking in preparation for Gran and Hamish's wedding, which was now only a week away. After a simple church ceremony they were having the reception at the village hall, with refreshments provided by family and friends. Ishbel was delighted with this arrangement, she liked to see the village hall being used. Lal just hoped she and Bel hadn't taken on too much of the catering.

However, time would tell. At least tomorrow was Saturday and Bel would be home from school. Gran was also due back form a visit to Glasgow, where she had gone to buy her wedding dress. Nothing too special it couldn't be used again for other occasions, she had assured Lal. Hamish had gone with her. He seemed like a new person since the engagement had been announced. He had taken a visit to Glasgow to stay with Peter and Sally calmly in his stride. Maybe the trip to Canada wouldn't be beyond him, after all.

Lal was weighing out the butter and flour when she heard a car draw up outside. She frowned. It was too early for the postman and Gran wasn't due back until the evening. She rinsed her hands and went to the door, still drying them on the towel.

Her heart did a strange little skip when she saw whose car it was. A dark, very clean four by four — with Iain Cunningham already climbing out of it.

Lal and Iain had only exchanged a couple of e-mails since her visit to Edinburgh, stilted polite communications that almost broke her heart. And now he was here!

'Hello,' she said cautiously. 'I wasn't expecting you.'

Iain nodded his head in acknow-ledgement of this. 'Is it all right if I come in?'

'Yes. Of course. Gran isn't here, she's been down in Glasgow for a few days.'

'Making preparations for the wed-ding, is she? It must be an exciting time for you all.'

Lal led the way back to the kitchen, glad to shut out the cold day. She wanted to ask, *but why are you here?* But couldn't bring herself to say the words. He had probably come to check progress on the roof at Harbour House.

'Have you come to see how the McMichaels are getting on?' she said as she moved the kettle to the middle of the Rayburn.

'Partly. And, of course, I have my invite for the wedding next Saturday.'

'So you're staying for the whole week, are you? You should have said, we could have made sure the Bothy was aired for you.'

'As Bel has pointed out to me more than once, Sandy built it so well it doesn't really need to be aired.'

Iain took a seat at the little kitchen table, looking around approvingly. 'Everything is just the same here,' he said.

'Yes. It is. I'm baking,' added Lal unnecessarily, gesturing to the ingredients.

'You don't mind if I stay and watch, do you? I can make my own drink, I don't want to hold you back.' Iain was so relaxed it was strange. Even when he had stayed at Tigh na Mara whilst his parents were in the Bothy, Lal didn't remember him making himself so at home. It was as though he had finally realised how things were done round here.

Lal told herself this was a good thing. She let him get on with making his coffee and went back to her Victoria sponge.

Iain began to tell her what he and his brother had found out about the disappearance of the money from the family business so many years ago. It was a fascinating story and Lal forgot to be nervous around him and began to ask questions.

'So it wasn't Sandy who stole the money? Bel will be so glad!'

'We can't be totally sure what happened, but we're certain that Sandy certainly didn't take anything for himself.'

'He wouldn't. He was a very kind man. He would have tried to look after his sister.'

'Did he ever mention her to you?'

Lal frowned, trying to remember. 'I don't think so. Although now you mention it, I seem to recall he had spent quite a lot of time in Spain in the past. I think he might even have spoken about considering settling there. That would fit in, wouldn't it? But he said once he had seen Harbour House and Strathan, there was nowhere else for him.'

She glanced accusingly at Iain, and was surprised when he said, 'Yes, I can understand that.'

'You can?' Lal slipped the baking tins into the oven and came to sit down beside him. 'Do you think you might keep Harbour House then, come here for holidays?' She felt her spirits lift.

'No, I don't think that.'

'Oh.' Her spirits plummeted again. 'You're going to sell? The McMichaels are doing an excellent job, I'm sure once the house is wind and water tight it will sell easily.'

'I'm not planning on selling it.'

Iain had pushed his chair back from the table and stretched out his long legs. He was wearing jeans and an open-necked shirt and although he could never look anything but tidy, it struck Lal that he really was far more casual than previously. He looked almost like he could belong out here.

'You don't mean..?' she sat forward, too scared to put the thought into words. 'What do you mean?'

'I mean I'm moving up here, to live. For good.' He smiled broadly, those beautiful dark eyes never leaving her face. 'I'm moving to Strathan.'

'But . . . ' Lal was momentarily speechless. He seemed unusually light-hearted, but this couldn't be a joke.

Could it? 'But you live in Edinburgh. You said . . . your career . . . I thought . . . '

'I changed my mind,' he said simply. 'I can do work from here, and that's what I intend to do. It won't be exactly the career I once imagined for myself, but I realise now a career isn't everything. It's being in the right place, going where your heart tells you to go. That's what matters.'

Lal found her hands were shaking and put them carefully in her lap. 'Yes, that's what Sandy said. He would be so pleased you've come to the same conclusion.'

'Although for me it's not just the place.' Iain sat up straight, no longer looking so relaxed. 'I'm coming to live at Harbour House whatever happens, because I've realised it's the right place for me. But the fact that you are living next door, well that is certainly part of the attraction. We maybe don't know each other very well and perhaps you aren't interested but . . . ' he tailed off, looking now so anxious the last bit of unhappiness in Lal's heart melted.

'Yes,' she said simply. 'I'm interested.'

'In me?'

'In you.'

He smiled then and took her hand. 'I'm serious about this, about us. I'm sure you'll need some time, but I want you to know that as far as I'm concerned, you're the one. I just hope . . . I just hope you might come to feel the same way about me.'

Lal let out the deep breath she hadn't realised she was holding. She leant forward and kissed him, very gently, on the lips. Her heart was full to overflowing. 'I already do,' she said. 'I already do.'

Then he returned her kiss.

It was only when he eventually pulled back that he frowned, and then sniffed the air. 'Is that burning I can smell?'

They both burst out laughing as Lal scrambled to rescue the sponge cake. It didn't matter. She could make plenty of other cakes, but there would never be another moment like this. She hadn't known it was possible to feel so happy. This was the beginning of the rest of her life. Her life at Culkien, with Iain.

A Double Celebration

It had been a wonderful wedding. Gran looked lovely in her new sea-green and silver dress and Hamish wore a kilt, and had had a haircut, and looked really quite smart. It seemed as though everyone from Strathan to Inverloch had come to the reception. Fortunately, half of them had contributed to the food and drink, so there were no shortages.

Lal's dad had 'given away' the bride and delivered a moving speech about how pleased he was for the happy couple.

Gran and Hamish had just set off on the first stage of their journey to Canada. People were starting to drift away and Lal was taking a much-needed rest. Bel slipped into the seat beside her.

'It's been good, hasn't it?'

'Yes, it's been perfect.' Lal was now reconciled to her gran's new life and couldn't understand why it had worried her so much at first. 'They both looked so happy.'

'Yes,' said Bel, nodding approvingly. 'And there are some other people who look pretty happy too. You and Iain Cunningham. Is something going on you're not telling us about?'

Lal smiled and hoped she wasn't blushing. 'It's great that he's coming to live in Strathan, isn't it?'

'Very good. I never thought he'd see sense so quickly. He was even making a serious attempt to learn some of the dances. He's going to fit right in.'

Lal nodded, watching the subject of their discussion as he made his way over to them with much-needed glasses of lemonade. He chatted to a couple of people as he passed. Lal didn't think he would ever be considered a local, but he was accepted.

Peter and Sally and Lal's brother, Anthony, came to join them a short while later. Sally suggested they should start tidying up, but Peter said they could worry about that tomorrow. Now everyone should relax and reflect on a very happy day.

'Are you sure you and Bel will be all right at Tigh na Mara?' asked Sally, for the tenth time. 'It seems the happy couple don't know exactly how long they'll be away. And winters up here can be very hard.'

'We'll be fine,' said Lal and Bel at the same time.

'They'll be fine,' agreed Ant. 'And if they need any heavy work done, they can always call on me.'

Bel snorted. 'Are you actually offering to work?'

'I'll be just next door, if they need anything,' said Iain.

'Yes, I have to say I'm pleased about that,' said Peter. 'Not that Lal isn't very capable, but it is a comfort to know there is a man nearby.'

'I can manage,' said Lal. She was, of course, delighted to have Iain so close at hand, but she wasn't going to let them get away with thinking she needed help. The Dunmore women were tough.

They could cope.

'Of course you can, if you have to,' said Iain. 'But fortunately you don't. Now, as everyone happens to be here, I wondered if it was the right time to make a little announcement of our own?'

He looked around at the family gathering. Lal knew she was definitely blushing now. They had agreed to wait until after Gran's wedding before telling people of their own plans. She hadn't expected it to be quite so soon after the wedding!

'You're getting married?' shrieked Bel.

'Goodness, isn't that a bit quick?' said Ant.

'Congratulations,' said Peter.

'Let them get a word in,' said Sally.

'Yes, we're getting married,' said Iain. Somehow he had managed to slip the ring they had bought secretly in Inverness onto her fourth finger. Now he lifted her hand to his lips and kissed it gently.

'We hope you'll be pleased,' said Lal, feeling rather breathless. 'We're thinking of a spring wedding, Harbour House should be ready by then, and . . . '

The rest of her words were lost in the excitement of hugs from the family, and then Bel racing around the hall to spread the news to everyone who hadn't yet left.

'And can I be a proper bridesmaid this time? I know Gran said it wasn't what she wanted, her being so old and that, but you can have a huge wedding, if the weather is good you can have the ceremony on the beach, oh this is going to be brilliant . . . '

It wouldn't have been Bel if she hadn't been bursting with ideas and intent on sharing them instantaneously.

Lal leant her head on Iain's shoulder. 'I hope you realise what you are letting yourself in for.'

'I realise,' he said happily, and bent to kiss her.

THE END

We do hope that you have enjoyed reading this large print book.

Did you know that all of our titles are available for purchase?

We publish a wide range of high quality large print books including:
Romances, Mysteries, Classics
General Fiction
Non Fiction and Westerns

Special interest titles available in large print are:
The Little Oxford Dictionary
Music Book, Song Book
Hymn Book, Service Book

Also available from us courtesy of Oxford University Press:
Young Readers' Dictionary
(large print edition)
Young Readers' Thesaurus
(large print edition)

For further information or a free brochure, please contact us at:
Ulverscroft Large Print Books Ltd.,
The Green, Bradgate Road, Anstey,
Leicester, LE7 7FU, England.
Tel: (00 44) **0116 236 4325**
Fax: (00 44) **0116 234 0205**

Other titles in the
Linford Romance Library:

WOMBAT CREEK

Noelene Jenkinson

Single mother Summer Dalton arrives from New South Wales to her grandfather's small farm in the Western District. However, memories of her hippy parents' banishment for their free-loving morals — decades before — remain. Her hope is to settle on the land she's inherited, so she refuses her new neighbour Ethan Bourke's offer to buy her out. Then, a jealous old flame and Ethan's disapproving mother come into the mix. Can Summer and Ethan resolve their growing attraction to one another?